MACMILLAN GUIDED REA
INTERMEDIATE LEVE

COLIN DEXTER

The Jewel That Was Ours

Retold by Anne Collins

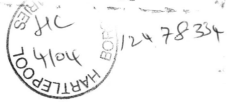

MACMILLAN
MODERNS

INTERMEDIATE LEVEL

Founding Editor: John Milne

Macmillan Guided Readers provide a choice of enjoyable reading material for all learners of English. The series comprises three categories: MODERNS, CLASSICS and ORIGINALS. Macmillan **Moderns** are retold versions of popular and contemporary novels, published at four levels of grading – Beginner, Elementary, Intermediate and Upper. At **Intermediate Level**, the control of content and language has the following main features:

Information Control

Information vital to the understanding of the story is presented in an easily assimilated manner and is repeated when necessary. Difficult allusion and metaphor are avoided and cultural backgrounds are made explicit.

Structure Control

Most structures used in the Readers will be familiar to students who have completed an elementary course of English. Other grammatical features may occur, but their use is made clear through context and reinforcement. This ensures that the reading is enjoyable and provides a continual learning situation for the students. Sentences are limited in most cases to a maximum of three clauses and within sentences there is a balance of adverbial and adjectival phrases. Great care is taken with pronoun reference.

Vocabulary Control

At **Intermediate Level** there is a basic vocabulary of approximately 1600 words. Help is given to students in the form of illustrations which are closely related to the text.

Glossary

Some difficult words and phrases in this book are important for understanding the story. Some of these words are explained in the story, some are shown in the pictures, and others are marked with a number like this: ...[1] Words with a number are explained in the Glossary.

Contents

A Note About This Story

Colin Dexter is one of Britain's most famous writers of detective stories. He has lived and worked in Oxford for many years. He has written thirteen novels about Inspector Morse and Sergeant Lewis. All of these novels, and many other stories about Morse, have been filmed for television, and these films have been seen in many countries.

In these stories, Morse and Lewis are members of the Thames Valley Police. There are many police forces in Britain. Each force works in a large area of the country. The Thames Valley Police is a real police force, and Oxford is one of the largest cities in its area. The headquarters of the police force is in a small town a few kilometres north of Oxford, but there is also a large police station in a street called St Aldate's, in the centre of Oxford. In this story Morse and Lewis work in both these places.

Morse and Lewis are not real policemen, and the events in this story never really happened. But most of the places in this story are real places. The Randolph Hotel is a real hotel. The University of Oxford is made up of many colleges, some large and some small. The ones which are mentioned in this story – St John's College, Balliol College, Trinity College and Magdalen College, are all real colleges. The University also has a famous library – the Bodleian Library – and a famous museum, the Ashmolean Museum. The library is named after a man called Bodley and the museum is named after a man called Ashmole. The chief of each department in the library or the museum is called the Keeper of that department. One of the people in this story is a Keeper at the Ashmolean Museum.

Two rivers run through Oxford, the Thames and the Cherwell. The Cherwell runs through the area of North Oxford. This is an area of expensive houses where many of the teachers in the university live.

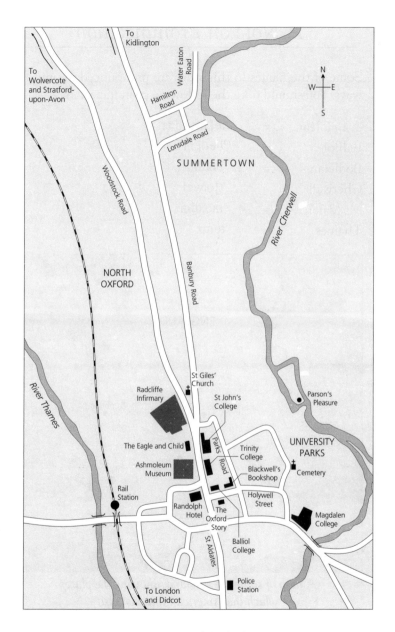

A Map of Oxford

A Note on Pronunciation

Some of the names in this story are pronounced in unusual ways. You should note the following pronunciations –

Ashmolean	=	æʃ'məʊliːən
Balliol	=	'beɪliːɒl
Bodleian	=	'bɒdliːən
Cherwell	=	'tʃɑːwel
Magdalen	=	'mɔːdlɪn
Thames	=	temz

A map of southern England, showing the places which the American tourists[1] visit

The People in This Story

Chief Inspector Morse

Sergeant Lewis

Sheila Williams

Dr Theodore Kemp

Cedric Downes

Marion Kemp

Lucy Downes

John Ashenden

Janet Roscoe

Laura and Eddie Stratton

Shirley and Howard Brown

Phil Aldrich

7

1

The Americans Arrive

It was early one Wednesday evening, at the end of October 1990. In the bedroom of a house in North Oxford, a man and a woman were thinking their own thoughts. They had spent the afternoon there, making love together. The man's name was Dr Theodore Kemp, the woman was Mrs Sheila Williams, and they were both lecturers[2] at Oxford University.

Outside, it was dark and heavy rain was falling. The rain beat against the window of the room. Sheila was standing by the window looking out at the wet street. In the rain, the street looked shiny and black.

Sheila turned her head and looked at Theodore Kemp, who was still lying in the bed. 'He's probably thinking about his wife, or about some other woman,' she thought sadly. 'I should tell him to get out of my bed and out of my life. But I can't do it. My husband has left me and I don't want to lose Theodore too.'

Kemp's dark moustache and beard formed a neat circle round his mouth. 'But his mouth is too small,' thought Sheila, 'and he's so arrogant – he thinks that he's very special and very clever.'

'I must go!' Kemp said suddenly. He sat up in the bed, swung his legs to the floor and picked up his shirt.

'Can we see each other tomorrow?' Sheila asked softly.

'Perhaps for a short time in the afternoon,' the man replied. 'But you know we'll be very busy with our group of Americans tomorrow evening. And then —'

'And then you must go home, of course.'

'Yes, of course! You know why. I have to go back to Marion.'

Sheila nodded. Kemp always had to go home to his wife.

Kemp dressed quickly, kissed Sheila lightly on the back of her neck and left the room. A moment later, she heard the sound of the street door closing. Feeling miserable, she watched the top of Kemp's black umbrella as he walked away down the street.

Kemp walked quickly through the rain to his flat, which was just a few minutes away. He was thinking that he ought to end his affair[3] with Sheila Williams. She was demanding more and more of his time. Also, she drank too much alcohol and she was putting on weight. And there *were* other women that he was interested in – one woman in particular.

―――

The following afternoon, a large, modern coach was approaching Oxford. The coach, which had come from Cambridge, contained a group of twenty-seven American tourists – nineteen women and eight men – who were the members of a tour group. The tour was called 'The Historic England Tour'.

The tour leader, John Ashenden, was sitting at the front of the coach. Ashenden's job was to look after the group, and to make sure that they had no problems at any of the hotels where they stayed. He also gave them information about interesting places and events in the historic towns and cities on the tour – London, Cambridge, Oxford, Stratford-upon-Avon[4], Bath and Winchester.

The tourists liked to sit in the same seats on the coach each day. As usual, Phil Aldrich, a small elderly man from California, was sitting by himself on the back seat. At the front of the coach, in the seat opposite Ashenden, was Mrs Janet Roscoe. Mrs Roscoe, a lady in her seventies, was also from California. She was the most difficult member of the group. She complained about everything – she was always looking for problems.

A married couple was sitting just behind Janet Roscoe. They were Eddie and Laura Stratton. As the coach passed a road sign pointing to Oxford city centre, Laura Stratton crossed her legs and rubbed her left foot. Then she turned to her husband.

'I feel terrible, Eddie,' she said in a loud voice. 'My feet are *really* hurting.' Laura suffered from arthritis[5] and this illness often caused terrible pains in her feet.

'Relax, honey[6],' said Eddie. 'Everything's going to be OK.'

After a moment, his wife smiled at him. 'Yes. I'll be fine, Ed,' she said. 'I'll be fine when we get to the hotel and I can have a bath.'

The coach was getting near the city centre now. Ashenden was speaking about the architecture[7] of the buildings which they could see.

'Do you see those iron gates?' he said. 'They are the entrance to the University Parks, a large area of parkland which belongs to Oxford University.'

The couple just behind Ashenden – Shirley and Howard Brown – looked out of the coach window at the University Parks. Howard Brown was feeling very excited. This was not the first time he had been in Oxford and he felt almost as if he was coming home. He was going to meet an old friend, but he had not told his wife about this.

One minute later, the coach stopped in front of the Randolph Hotel, the most famous hotel in Oxford.

'At last!' said Laura Stratton. 'Now I can rest my feet.'

Ashenden told the Americans to go inside immediately and get the keys to their rooms from the reception desk[8]. As soon as the receptionist had given Eddie Stratton his key – the key to Room 310 – Laura grabbed it from his hand.

'I'm going straight up to our room to have a bath – I can't wait any longer!' she said.

As soon as the receptionist had given Eddie Stratton his key,
Laura grabbed it from his hand.

'All right, honey, but leave the door open for me,' Eddie replied. 'You've got the only key. I'll go and have a cup of tea in the lounge and I'll come up to the room a little later.'

As Laura walked slowly and painfully towards the lift, Eddie turned and looked into the eyes of Mrs Shirley Brown. Shirley glanced quickly at her husband, then nodded at Eddie and smiled.

———

When Laura Stratton reached Room 310, she put the key in the lock and opened the door. She went inside the room, leaving the door slightly open as her husband had asked.

Room 310 was a very pleasant and comfortable room. Near the door was a double bed with a small table beside it. Laura was carrying her white leather handbag. She put it down carefully on the table. Then she sat down on the bed and removed the shoes from her tired, painful feet.

She went into the bathroom and turned on the hot tap. Next, she came back into the bedroom, picked up a DO NOT DISTURB sign[9] and hung it on the outside of the door. Finally, she returned to the bathroom and poured some pink bubble bath[10] into the hot water.

At that moment, Laura Stratton did not know that she had only a few more minutes to live.

———

A cleaner had been working in the corridor outside Room 310 at 4.40 that afternoon. Later, the police interviewed the cleaner and asked her lots of questions about what she had seen there. The cleaner had a very good memory and she was able to answer all their questions.

She told them that she had seen Laura Stratton go into the room by herself. Then at 4.45 p.m. she had noticed the DO NOT DISTURB sign hanging on the outside of the door. She had wondered why the door was slightly open if the woman did not want to be disturbed. But when she looked into the room, she saw steam coming from the bathroom. Someone was having a bath, so she had not looked any further. But she was quite sure that there had been no white leather handbag on the small table next to the bed.

———

John Ashenden walked out of the Randolph Hotel at 4.45, crossed the road and turned into Broad Street. The early evening air was cool, so he walked quickly. He passed Balliol College, the south gate of Trinity College and Blackwell's famous bookshop, and waited for some cars to pass before he crossed Parks Road. As he was waiting, he saw two people standing on the other side of the road. He recognised them at once, but when the cars had passed he hurried on.

He walked quickly down Holywell Street and at the end, he turned left. After about a hundred metres, there was a wooden gate which led into an old cemetery. Many famous people from Oxford were buried in Holywell Cemetery.

Ashenden walked along a curving path through the cemetery. Then he stopped, and started to look for something in the long grass. He searched for nearly twenty minutes before he found what he was looking for. It was a small, low tombstone[11] with a few words carved on it.

JAMES ALFRED BOWDEN
1956 – 1981
REST IN PEACE

Ashenden stood looking at the stone for several minutes. He was remembering James Bowden. When he was a young man, James had been his dearest friend. They had lost touch[12], but Ashenden had never forgotten him.

Ashenden looked around him. There was nobody else in

13

the cemetery. Quickly, he divided the long grass at the bottom of the tombstone. He pulled something out of his pocket and put it at the bottom of the stone. Then he replaced the plants so that nobody could see what he had done.

It was getting dark. He left the cemetery and walked back to the Randolph Hotel.

––––

As Eddie Stratton and Shirley Brown walked back to the hotel, they were talking about John Ashenden. They had seen him walking down Holywell Street, but they didn't know whether he'd seen them.

'I want to know where he was going,' said Shirley. 'He was walking very quickly and looking around him carefully. He didn't want anybody to see him.'

'Do you think that he saw us?' asked Eddie.

'Yes,' replied Shirley. 'I think that he did.'

When they got back to the hotel, they went upstairs in the lift together.

'I'll see you later, Shirl,' said Eddie as he walked towards Room 310.

'Yes,' said Shirley. 'I hope that Laura's feet are better.'

2

A Death and a Theft

Later that afternoon, the manager of the Randolph Hotel phoned St Aldate's Police Station in Oxford. He said that somebody had died at the hotel, and that there had been a theft[13] from her room. As a result of this call, Chief Inspector

Morse was sent to the Randolph with his assistant, Sergeant Lewis. Morse was a very clever detective – the cleverest in the Thames Valley Police Force. He'd solved many difficult crimes and Sergeant Lewis had worked with him on most of these cases[14].

When Morse and Lewis arrived at the hotel, they immediately went up to Room 310. Mrs Laura Stratton was lying on the bed, wearing a dressing gown. Morse saw at once that she was dead.

A young man with a pink face was sitting at a table in the room, writing. He was the hotel doctor. Before Morse could say anything, the doctor turned his head and spoke to the detective.

'She died from a heart attack[15].'

'Thank you, Dr — ?' said Morse.

'Dr Swain. And you are?'

'Morse. I'm Chief Inspector Morse.'

Dr Swain handed Morse a sheet of paper. 'Here's my report,' he said. 'There's no doubt about the cause of this woman's death. And now I really have to go. I have to attend a very important dinner this evening.'

Morse decided that he did not like Swain. The doctor spoke and behaved in a very arrogant way, as if he was cleverer than anybody else.

'I'm sorry, Doctor, but you can't leave yet,' said Morse. 'Two things have happened here – not only a death, but also a theft. I understand that something very valuable has been stolen from this room.'

'The manager only told me about the theft five minutes ago,' Dr Swain replied. 'But the theft wasn't the cause of this woman's death. She died from a heart attack. I've already told you that.'

'Did she die on the bed?'

'No – she died on the floor.'

'You moved her body!' said Morse angrily. 'Why did you do that? You might have destroyed some important evidence[16]. This woman might have been murdered by the thief.'

'But she *wasn't* murdered!' said Dr Swain. Now he was angry too. 'I've *told* you – she died of a heart attack.'

'All right, Doctor,' said Morse calmly. 'You don't have to tell me everything three times. You can go to your dinner now. But I am going to ask the police pathologist[17] to come here and look at this dead body.'

'But that's not necessary —' began Dr Swain. Then he stopped.

Morse did not say anything else. He didn't want to talk to Dr Swain any more. Silently, he held the door of Room 310 open for the doctor to leave.

———

Eddie Stratton, the dead woman's husband, was sitting in the hotel manager's office. Morse was interviewing him there. Eddie was a tall, sun-tanned Californian and Morse liked him immediately. But Eddie did not seem very sad about his wife's death – there was no sign of tears on his face.

Eddie told Morse that when his wife had gone up to their room, he had gone out for a walk with another lady from the tour. The lady's name was Mrs Shirley Brown. They had both wanted to stretch their legs[18] after the coach journey. They had returned to the hotel at about 5.20 p.m. and Eddie had immediately gone up to Room 310. But the door to the room had been shut, and when he'd knocked on it, Laura had not replied. So he'd gone downstairs again to the hotel reception desk to get another key.

When he'd finally entered the room, Eddie Stratton had found his wife Laura lying dead on the carpet. And he'd quickly noticed that her handbag was missing.

'Your wife was dead, but the first thing you thought about was her handbag?' asked Morse. 'That's rather strange, isn't it?'

'No, it isn't, Inspector,' replied Eddie Stratton. 'You see, there was something very valuable in that handbag.'

———

That evening, there was a party to welcome the group of American tourists. It was held in the St John's Suite, one of the finest rooms of the Randolph Hotel. At 6.45 p.m. Sheila Williams was standing with a large glass of wine in her hand, looking at the visitors. Sheila was the only person in the room at that moment who had been told about Laura Stratton's death. Eddie Stratton was not at the party and neither were Howard and Shirley Brown.

Three lecturers from Oxford University were going to give talks to the group while they were in Oxford. The lecturers were Sheila Williams herself, Dr Theodore Kemp and another lecturer, called Cedric Downes. They would all be at the party. Kemp had not yet arrived, but Cedric Downes stood talking with some of the Americans.

At about 7.25 p.m., Dr Kemp came in with Ashenden, the tour leader. Both of them looked very serious. Sheila guessed that they had been told about Laura Stratton's death. She looked at Kemp and he smiled at her.

———

'Ladies and gentlemen,' said Sheila loudly a few minutes later, talking to everyone in the room. 'Mr Ashenden has asked me to talk to you about the programme for your visit to Oxford. Please look at your programme sheets.' Ashenden had earlier prepared a list of the programme details on pieces of yellow paper. Each person in the group had been given one of these yellow 'sheets'.

HISTORIC ENGLAND TOUR

27th October – 10th November 1990

PROGRAMME FOR OUR STAY IN OXFORD

Thursday 1st November

4.30 p.m.	We arrive at the Randolph Hotel.
4.30–5.30	Tea in the hotel lounge.
6.45	Welcome party (St John's Suite). Mrs Sheila Williams will talk about the programme. After that, Mr Cedric Downes will give a talk about 'The Buildings of Oxford'.
8.00	Dinner in the hotel dining-room.
9.30–10.30	Dr Theodore Kemp will give a talk about 'The Treasures of the Ashmolean Museum'.

Friday 2nd November

7.30–9.15 a.m.	Breakfast in the dining-room.
10.30–11.30	Visit to 'The Oxford Story' exhibition in Broad Street (100 metres from the hotel).
11.30–12.45	Free time.
12.45 p.m.	Lunch in the St John's Suite.
3.00	We divide into three groups. Details will be given later.
4.30–5.30	Tea in the hotel lounge.
6.30	Mrs Laura Stratton will present the Wolvercote Tongue to the Ashmolean Museum.
8.00	Dinner.

Saturday 3rd November

7.30–8.30 a.m.	Breakfast.
9.30	We leave Oxford to travel to Stratford-upon-Avon.

Sheila spoke for ten minutes, explaining the programme in greater detail. 'And now,' she said, 'it's my great pleasure to introduce Mr Cedric Downes. Mr Downes is going to talk to you about the architecture of Oxford.'

'Thank you, Sheila,' said Downes. 'Most visitors to Oxford think that all our buildings are old. We do have wonderful old buildings here, and I'll talk about some of them later. But we have some very interesting modern buildings too. Some good examples are —'

Just then the door opened and a stranger came in. The group stared at him in surprise.

'Is Mrs Sheila Williams here?' the stranger asked.

Sheila raised her hand. The man walked over to her.

'Could I talk to you privately, please?' he asked quietly. 'I'm Sergeant Lewis from the Thames Valley Police.'

———

Morse was waiting in the hotel manager's office. He looked up as Lewis brought Sheila into the room. He saw a very attractive woman in her mid thirties. She had lovely dark brown eyes. But she looked slightly drunk.

'Please sit down, Mrs Williams,' Morse said. 'I want you to tell me about these American tourists. I'll need to ask everybody in the tour group some questions. I want to know what each of them was doing this afternoon between about four thirty and five fifteen. Mr Stratton last saw his wife alive at four thirty. When he returned from his walk at five fifteen, she was dead and her handbag was missing.'

'But most of the tour group don't know yet that Mrs Stratton is dead,' said Sheila.

'No. We'll tell them after dinner,' Morse replied. 'Now, please tell me about the people on the tour.'

'Well,' said Sheila, 'most of them are from California. The tour is very expensive, so everybody on it must be quite

19

rich. Most of them, but not all of them, have visited England before.'

'What can you tell me about the dead woman, Mrs Laura Stratton?'

'Mrs Stratton had a special reason for coming to Oxford. She was bringing something very valuable with her – the Wolvercote Tongue.'

'And what is the Wolvercote Tongue?' asked Morse. 'I've never heard of it.'

'The Wolvercote Tongue is part of an extremely valuable artefact[19] – a very old and beautiful jewel. It was made from gold and precious stones in the eighth century. The other part of the artefact is called the Wolvecote Buckle. The Wolvercote Tongue fits into the Wolvercote Buckle, and together they make the complete jewel,' she went on. 'The Tongue is in the shape of a pear. It once had three large rubies[20] in it, but there is only one left now.

'For some reason, the two parts of the artefact became separated,' Sheila continued. 'The Buckle was found in Wolvercote in the 1930s.' Morse nodded. The small village of Wolvercote was very close to Oxford.

'The Wolvercote Buckle is kept in the Ashmolean Museum,' Sheila said. Morse nodded again. The Ashmolean was the University Museum, just across the street from the Randolph.

'But why did Laura Stratton have the Wolvercote Tongue?' asked Morse.

'Eddie Stratton is Laura's second husband. Her first husband, Cyrus Palmer, died two years ago. He was a collector of antiquities[21], and the Wolvercote Tongue was part of his collection. I don't know where he got it – perhaps he bought it from someone in London. But when he died, he left the Tongue to the Ashmolean Museum in his will[22]. He wanted it to be kept in the museum together with the Buckle. He wanted the two parts of the jewel to be joined again.'

'I see,' said Morse. 'So Mrs Stratton was bringing the Wolvercote Tongue from America to the Ashmolean Museum in Oxford.'

'Yes,' replied Sheila. 'She was going to present it to Dr Kemp[23] in a special ceremony tomorrow afternoon. Dr Kemp is the Keeper of Antiquities at the Ashmolean Museum. The presentation of the Tongue to the Museum was very important to him.'

'Where did Mrs Stratton keep this jewel?' asked Lewis.

'Her husband told me that she always carried it in her handbag,' replied Sheila. 'She didn't want to be separated from it because it was so valuable.'

'And now somebody has stolen the handbag,' said Morse. He stared at Sheila thoughtfully. As the inspector did not say anything else, Lewis asked, 'What about you, Mrs Williams? What were *you* doing between four thirty and five fifteen this afternoon?'

Suddenly Sheila began to cry. Morse and Lewis were very surprised. Why was she so upset? When she replied, she spoke only a few words.

'Ask Dr Kemp – he'll explain!'

Morse was angry that Lewis had made Sheila cry, so he told her that she was free to go. Sheila left the room without answering Lewis's question.

3

'But This Wasn't Murder!'

Morse was still sitting in the hotel manager's office. He was thinking about Laura Stratton's death, and the theft of the Wolvercote Tongue. He was sure that the two things were connected – there had to be a link between them. The inspector looked up when the police pathologist came into the room.

'Well, Max?' said Morse. 'Have you examined Mrs Stratton's body?'

'Yes,' replied Max. 'But there's nothing here for the police to investigate, Morse. This wasn't murder. The woman died from a heart attack.'

'So Doctor Swain was right,' said Morse.

'Yes,' said Max. 'Don't start looking for any murderers.'

When Max had gone, Morse sat alone for a few more minutes. He had been wrong. Nobody had murdered Laura Stratton. There was still a crime to solve – the theft of the Wolvercote Tongue – but Morse felt disappointed. He always enjoyed trying to catch a murderer, but he was not really interested in thieves. Suddenly Morse felt tired. All he wanted to do was go back to his flat and listen to some music. But just then, Lewis came in with Dr Theodore Kemp.

Morse felt an immediate dislike towards Kemp. Kemp was in his late thirties and he had a beard. He seemed to be a typical 'Oxford University man' – he looked clever but he looked arrogant too. Morse guessed that he was proud of being cleverer then other people.

'What can you tell us about the Wolvercote Tongue?' Morse asked him.

Kemp was carrying a black briefcase[24]. He opened it and took out a pile of pale-blue leaflets, and handed one each to

Morse and Lewis.

'This is the information that I prepared for the group,' he said.

Morse quickly read the leaflet.

The Wolvercote Jewel

In 1931, an exciting discovery was made in the village of Wolvercote near Oxford. A gold buckle was found, which had been made in the eighth century. Since its discovery, the Wolvercote Buckle has been kept in the Ashmolean Museum.

More recently, another exciting discovery has been made. We know now that the Wolvercote Buckle is only half of an eighth-century jewel. The other half, which is now called the Wolvercote Tongue, was for some years in the collection of Cyrus Palmer, of Pasadena in California. When Mr Palmer died recently, he left the Tongue to the Ashmolean Museum. Mrs Laura Stratton, Mr Palmer's widow, is going to present the Tongue to the museum at a small ceremony on November 2nd.

When the Buckle and the Tongue are joined together again, the whole artefact will be known as The Wolvercote Jewel. What was the purpose of this Jewel? Perhaps it was once part of the cloak of an ancient king. Perhaps it was used in important ceremonies. We will never really know.

But one thing is certain – with its parts joined together again, the Wolvercote Jewel will be one of the Ashmolean Museum's finest treasures.

'You wrote this yourself, sir?' Morse asked when he had finished reading.

Kemp nodded. He was angry. He had been thinking for months about the presentation of the Wolvercote Tongue to the Ashmolean Museum. It would have been the most important moment of his career as Keeper of Antiquities at the museum. His name would have been in the newspapers and his face would have been on television. He was going to write a book about the Tongue. And now the presentation had been cancelled because the Tongue was missing.

'What were you doing today between four thirty and five fifteen?' asked Morse.

'I don't know!' replied Kemp angrily. 'I was probably in the Ashmolean, preparing for the presentation. But I don't know and I don't care! Nothing matters now!'

He stood up, grabbed the leaflets, and tore them into pieces. Then he threw them down on the desk and went out. Morse let him go. The detective was thinking. Sheila Williams had not answered Lewis's question, and now Kemp had not answered his own question.

'You didn't like him much, did you, sir?' asked Lewis.

'No,' said Morse. 'But he didn't steal the Wolvercote Tongue. The presentation was very important for him. And now the Tongue has gone and his career has been damaged.'

Suddenly Morse felt bored with the Wolvercote Tongue.

'Tell the undertaker[25] to move Laura Stratton's body out of the hotel,' he said to Lewis. 'Then go and interview the rest of the tour group and ask each person what they were doing this afternoon.'

'Aren't we going to search the hotel rooms, sir?' asked Lewis.

'Search the rooms? Of course not! Do you know how many rooms there are in the Randolph?'

24

He stood up, grabbed the leaflets, and tore them into pieces.

Before Morse left the Randolph, he decided to have a drink in the bar. Sheila Williams was sitting there with John Ashenden. When she saw Morse, Sheila waved to him.

'Inspector Morse! Come and join us!' she called.

Morse smiled and went over to Sheila.

'Inspector, this is John Ashenden – he's the tour leader. We were just talking about what he was doing this afternoon. John went out to visit one of the colleges when the coach arrived here, didn't you, John?'

'Yes,' said Ashenden. 'I went to visit Magdalen College. It's a wonderful place. It has a park full of deer. You can go for a beautiful walk by the River Cherwell – there's a huge area of fields and gardens. And the college tower is one of the finest towers in Europe.'

As Ashenden spoke, Morse looked at him in surprise. Later, as he walked back to his flat, Morse was thinking. He had become interested in the case again.

'Laura Stratton died of a heart attack in her hotel room between four thirty and five fifteen,' he thought. 'Her husband was taking a walk with another woman at that time. When Eddie Stratton returned to the hotel, he found his wife dead. And he says that her handbag – with a valuable jewel inside – is missing.

'The Wolvercote Tongue is a very special artefact and it would be difficult for a thief to sell it. But perhaps it's insured[26] for a large amount of money. If it's lost or stolen, the insurance company would have to pay a lot of money to the owners. Perhaps Laura and Eddie Stratton needed money. Perhaps they *wanted* the Tongue to be stolen. Perhaps they arranged the theft themselves.

'Perhaps the Wolvercote Tongue wasn't in Laura Stratton's handbag at all,' Morse thought. 'Perhaps it never left America!'

4

Oxford Stories

Theodore Kemp and Cedric Downes were very different kinds of men.

To most people, Theodore Kemp seemed more successful than Cedric Downes. He was younger than Downes and he spoke in a beautiful voice. He dressed well, and he was always smart and neat. He liked women and many of them found him attractive too. He had had many girlfriends before his marriage, and now he was having an affair with Sheila Williams.

Cedric Downes was not like Kemp at all. Downes was middle-aged and slightly heavy. He had long, dark hair and his clothes were untidy. He was going deaf in his left ear and sometimes wore a hearing-aid. This was a small plastic object placed in his ear which made sounds clearer for him.

But many things had not gone well for Theodore Kemp, and Cedric Downes was the luckier man.

Kemp had married a woman called Marion. Marion was not pretty, but her parents were rich. That was why Kemp had married her. Two years before, when Marion was pregnant, she and Kemp had been involved in a terrible car accident. Kemp, who had been driving the car, was not hurt. But Marion's unborn baby had died and she had lost the use of her legs. Since the accident, her legs had been completely paralysed and she could not walk. The only way she could move very far was by using a wheelchair[27].

In the accident, the Kemps' car had crashed into another car. The driver of that car, a thirty-five-year-old woman, had been killed. It could not be proved which driver was responsible for the accident – nobody could really say whose fault the accident was. But Kemp had been drinking and there was alcohol in his blood. So he had to pay a large fine[28] and his driving licence was taken away for three years.

Many of Kemp's colleagues[29] at the University thought that he was very lucky – a woman had been killed and Kemp had not gone to prison. But after the accident, things did not go well for Kemp. When he applied for better jobs at the University, he was unsuccessful.

Marion Kemp could no longer go up and down stairs. So the Kemps had had to move from their beautiful large house to a ground-floor flat. The flat was small, modern and not very attractive. It was in a building called Cherwell Lodge, in Water Eaton Road in North Oxford. The Kemps hated it.

Cedric Downes was married too. He had married one of his students – an attractive young woman called Lucy – who was eleven years younger than Downes. Lucy had blonde hair and beautiful skin and, unlike Marion Kemp, she was very healthy. The Downeses also lived in North Oxford. They lived in a large, beautiful house in Lonsdale Road, about 300 metres from the Kemps' house. Its lovely garden sloped down to the banks of the River Cherwell.

———

On the day of Laura Stratton's death, Theodore Kemp arrived home at about 10 p.m. Marion was lying in bed – she spent a lot of her time lying in bed and thinking. For a long time, she had been feeling very angry with her husband. She knew that he was having an affair with Sheila Williams. Now she hated her husband and she hated Sheila Williams.

Kemp immediately told Marion about the theft of the Wolvercote Tongue. She understood why he was very upset about the loss of the jewel. He had lost his chance of being famous, and perhaps his chance of getting a better job in the University.

Later, Marion lay awake thinking about her husband. She could not sleep. She suspected[30] that Theodore was losing interest in Sheila Williams. But she also suspected that he was becoming interested in another woman.

And she thought she knew who this other woman was.

———

When Cedric Downes arrived home that evening, his wife Lucy was already in bed. She looked as if she was asleep. When he got into bed, he pressed his body against her, but she did not move. For a few minutes Downes thought about the events of the day. But he was very tired and soon he was in a deep sleep.

But Lucy Downes was only pretending to be asleep. She lay in the dark, breathing quietly and thinking.

———

The next morning, the Americans were having breakfast at the Randolph Hotel. Mrs Janet Roscoe, the most difficult member of the group, was drinking a cup of black coffee. She watched Phil Aldrich enjoying a very large 'English Breakfast' – bacon, sausages and eggs.

'I don't know how you can eat all that food,' she said loudly. 'And it isn't healthy food.'

Phil continued eating happily. He smiled at the other tourists.

'I've known Janet a long time,' he told them.

Then Ashenden came to tell the group that there was going to be a meeting in the St John's Suite at 9.15. He had already informed everybody about Laura Stratton's death, and now he explained that the rest of the tour would continue as planned. This was what Eddie Stratton wanted.

———

In the St John's Suite, Ashenden talked to the group about their yellow tour sheets with the programme details.

'There are a few small changes in the details for today,' he said. 'It says on the sheets that we are going to visit

The Oxford Story at ten thirty. But now this visit has been put back to ten o'clock.'

'Don't you mean "brought forward" to ten o'clock, Mr Ashenden?' said Janet Roscoe at once. 'Ten o'clock is *earlier* than ten thirty.'

Ashenden sighed. 'You're right, Mrs Roscoe,' he replied. 'I mean "brought forward". I'm sorry.'

Ashenden handed each member of the group a piece of paper with information about The Oxford Story.

The Oxford Story

Many wonderful and important things have happened here in Oxford. The Oxford Story is an exhibition about the city's place in history and in literature. As you sit comfortably in a moving seat, you will be taken on a journey that tells Oxford's history through the centuries.

'You'll leave The Oxford Story at about eleven fifteen,' Ashenden continued. 'After that, there is another change to the programme. There will be a special "Question and Answer" discussion, when Mrs Williams, Mr Downes and Dr Kemp will answer all your questions about Oxford. This will take us through to lunch at about twelve thirty.

'Unfortunately, for reasons that you already know, the presentation of the Wolvercote Tongue to the Ashmolean Museum has been cancelled. But we are still going to divide into groups earlier in the afternoon. Can we please meet at two forty-five, not at three o'clock? Dr Kemp will meet his group outside the Ashmolean Museum, Mr Downes will meet his group outside Blackwell's Bookshop and Mrs Williams will meet her group at the hotel reception desk.'

'Don't you mean "brought forward" to ten o'clock?'
said Janet Roscoe at once.

'There is only one other change,' Ashenden went on. 'Dinner has been *brought forward* – is that right, Mrs Roscoe? – from eight o'clock to seven thirty. Are there any questions?'

The Americans shook their heads. They were all quite happy with the day's programme – even, it seemed, Mrs Roscoe.

5

Theodore Kemp Disappears

At 9.50 a.m., Cedric Downes led the group of Americans down the steps of the Randolph Hotel. They crossed the road, to the tall building which contained the exhibition called The Oxford Story. He left them there and walked down the street to Blackwell's Bookshop. After he had spent some time in the shop, he decided to go back to the hotel.

As Downes was entering the hotel, he heard someone shouting.

'Cedric!'

He turned and saw Sheila Williams.

'You must be deaf,' she said loudly. 'I called you three or four times.'

'I *am* deaf, Sheila,' said Cedric, smiling.

'Have you got time for a drink before the group gets back?' asked Sheila. She looked at her watch. It was just after eleven o'clock.

'Yes, please, Sheila,' he said.

They walked into the hotel bar together, ordered two drinks and sat down on a large sofa.

A few minutes later, Ashenden came in.

'Hello, you two,' he said. 'I thought that you'd be here.'

'Is there any news of the Wolvercote Tongue?' asked Downes.

Ashenden shook his head.

'No. Nobody seems to be very hopeful about finding it.'

'Poor Theo!' said Sheila. 'He's very upset about the theft.'

'I have something to tell you,' Ashenden said. He was looking very uncomfortable. 'Dr Kemp won't be joining us this morning, I'm afraid.'

'Why not?' asked Sheila angrily. 'He's meant to be at the "Question and Answer" discussion with Cedric and me.'

'His wife phoned me earlier this morning. She said that Dr Kemp had gone to London. He has to see his publishers about a book he's writing.'

'That's typical of Theo!' said Sheila. 'That's just the selfish kind of behaviour that you can expect from him. He goes off to London and leaves me and Cedric to do all the hard work.'

'I'm really sorry, Sheila,' said John Ashenden. 'But he'll be back here at lunchtime. He'll be here in time to take his group round the Ashmolean Museum this afternoon.'

———

At 10.15 on that same morning, Inspector Morse was talking to Sergeant Lewis in his office at the Thames Valley Police Headquarters.

'Well, Lewis? Have you arrested the thief yet?' he asked his old friend.

Lewis shook his head. He was not in the mood for Morse's jokes today. He had spent a long time interviewing the group of Americans. He had asked them all what they were doing between four thirty and five fifteen the previous afternoon. He had written down all their statements – the things that each person had told him – and he was trying to sort out the information.

'Dr Kemp won't be joining us this morning,
I'm afraid,' said Ashenden.

'So did you learn anything interesting?' asked Morse.

'Not really,' replied Lewis. 'These Americans – well, some of them – couldn't remember exactly what they were doing at that time. But they all unpacked their clothes, drank tea, watched TV – that kind of thing. Everybody seemed to be telling the truth.'

'Except one,' said Morse.

'Really, sir? Who do you mean?'

'Ashenden,' Morse replied. 'John Ashenden was lying.'

Lewis looked surprised. 'How do you know that?'

'He said that he took a walk round Magdalen College. He told me all about it. But he was really giving a description of the college from a famous guidebook about Oxford. I know it well. He used almost the same words that appear in the book.

'That made me suspicious[31],' Morse went on. 'I phoned the College this morning. There are building repairs happening there and the College was closed to visitors all day yesterday.'

'Oh,' said Lewis sadly, looking down at all the statements on his desk. He had worked hard to get them, but they all seemed useless now. Morse was so clever. With just one phone call, the inspector had got more useful information than he himself had got in a whole evening.

'So Ashenden was telling lies,' said Lewis. 'Do you want me to arrest him?'

'You can't arrest a man for telling lies, Lewis. Perhaps Ashenden has a girlfriend in Oxford and he doesn't want anybody to find out about her. I don't know where he was yesterday afternoon. But one thing is certain. He wasn't at the Randolph Hotel stealing handbags.'

A few minutes later, Morse got into his car and drove towards North Oxford.

———

Cedric Downes and Sheila Williams answered all the group's questions very clearly in the 'Question and Answer' discussion. After that, everybody sat down to lunch in the St John's Suite.

At about 12.35, the hotel receptionist took a phone call. Later, when the police interviewed her about this call, she was able to answer their questions very clearly. She had written down the name of the person who called, on her notepad. It was Dr Theodore Kemp, and the person he asked to speak to was Mr John Ashenden. So she put the call through to the St John's Suite. Ashenden took the call on a phone close to Janet Roscoe's table.

After speaking to Dr Kemp, John Ashenden called the hotel reception desk and asked for a taxi to go to Oxford Station later that afternoon. The driver was asked to meet the train from London and to pick up Dr Theodore Kemp. The train would arrive in Oxford at 3.00 p.m.

———

Lewis stayed in his office for the rest of the morning. At 1.20 p.m., he took a bus to the centre of Oxford and got off near the Randolph Hotel. As he approached the hotel, he saw Sheila Williams walking quickly away from it. She did not see Sergeant Lewis.

Suddenly a man hurried down the steps of the Randolph. He looked back over his shoulder, then walked quickly along the street towards Oxford Station.

Lewis recognised the man at once. It was Eddie Stratton. But where was he going in such a hurry? Lewis started to follow him.

———

Later that afternoon, at 3.20 p.m., Cedric Downes was taking a group of the tourists round St John's College. At the same time, Sheila Williams was showing another group some old photographs in the Bodleian Library. But there was no third group in the Ashmolean Museum with Dr Theodore Kemp. Dr Kemp had still not come back to the hotel.

Some of the people who had been going to visit the museum joined one of the other groups. Some – like Mrs Janet Roscoe – said that they were tired and wanted to rest.

———

The University Parks in Oxford close every evening when the sun goes down. But for more than a hundred years, the Parks have been a popular place for young lovers to go after dark. It is not difficult to get in when the gates are locked!

That evening at 9.30, two young lovers had entered the Parks. They had crossed the Rainbow Bridge over the River Cherwell, and they were in an area of the Parks called Parson's Pleasure[32], just beyond the bridge. There were small cubicles there – changing-rooms where people could leave their clothes when they swam in the river. The young couple sat down in one of the cubicles, but it was cold and damp and uncomfortable.

'Please let's go!' the girl said to her boyfriend. 'I'm cold and I don't like it here.'

They left the cubicle and walked quickly back over the Rainbow Bridge. The water of the River Cherwell was very high and the river was flowing fast. The moon shone brightly on the water.

There was a weir[33] in front of them. It closed off part of the river to make an area for swimming. Suddenly the girl noticed something which was caught on top of the weir. It was pale and long and white and it looked terrible in the moonlight.

She screamed.

6

The Body in The Parks

Morse was at home, listening to music. It was getting late. Earlier in the evening, Lewis had phoned him.

'Eddie Stratton went to the railway station at lunchtime,' the sergeant had told Morse. 'He still hasn't returned to the Randolph.'

Now the phone rang again. Lewis had some more news. He said that a dead man had been found in the University Parks. The body was naked. The death was suspicious.

———

Morse went to the Parks at once. Lewis and Max, the police pathologist, were already there. The pathologist had just finished examining the body.

'The body was lying face down in the water,' Max said. 'There must have been a lot of blood from the wounds[34], but the river has washed him clean.'

'Who is it, Max?' asked Morse quietly.

'You're the detective, Morse!' the man replied. 'Guess!'

Morse knew that Eddie Stratton had not returned to the Randolph. Was he upset about the death of his wife? Had he jumped into the River Cherwell and killed himself?

'OK, I'll guess,' said Morse. 'I think that it's the body of a seventy-year-old Californian, a man called Eddie Stratton – the husband of the woman who died yesterday.'

'No, Morse, you're wrong,' said Max. 'This man wasn't in his seventies. He was probably in his forties. Look!'

The body was lying on the ground, under a cover. Max pulled back the cover and Morse stared at the body in surprise.

It was Dr Theodore Kemp.

———

As Max was putting his bag away in his car, Morse asked, 'What was the cause of Kemp's death, Max?'

'A wound to his head. It was made before he entered the water.'

'It wasn't suicide?' asked Morse. 'He didn't kill himself?'

'Oh, no,' replied Max.

'How long was he in the water?'

'It's difficult to say – perhaps between four and eight hours.'

When Max had gone, Morse turned to Lewis.

'You told me, Lewis, that Eddie Stratton was missing. So I thought that this was Eddie Stratton's body.'

'But I also told you, sir, that Dr Kemp was missing,' Lewis replied. 'Ashenden told me that he had arranged for a taxi to meet Dr Kemp's train at three o'clock. But Dr Kemp wasn't at the station.'

Morse decided to drive to the Randolph Hotel and find Ashenden. And there was another reason to visit the hotel. The bar would still be open and Morse needed a drink.

After Morse had gone, Lewis stayed at Parson's Pleasure to look for more evidence. And he found something very interesting on the ground near the changing cubicles. It was a sheet of yellow paper with details of the American group's tour programme. A change to the final time of that day's dinner had been written in by hand.

| 6.30 | Mrs Laura Stratton will present the Wolvercote Tongue to the Ashmolean Museum. |
| ~~8.00~~ 7.30 | Dinner. |

Saturday 3rd November

'So somebody from the American group was at Parson's Pleasure today, and dropped this programme,' thought Lewis. 'That's very interesting!'

Morse found Ashenden sitting at a table in the bar of the Randolph Hotel. Three other members of the group were with him – Howard and Shirley Brown, and Phil Aldrich. They were all very worried about Eddie Stratton and they were wondering where he was. Morse bought himself a drink and sat down with them. But he did not tell them about the death of Dr Kemp.

Later, Lewis called Morse at the hotel. He told Morse that Marion Kemp had phoned a police station. She had told an officer that her husband had left for London that morning, but he had still not come home.

When Morse went back to the bar, Phil Aldrich asked. 'Is there any news about Eddie, Inspector?'

'No,' said Morse.

A few minutes later, Morse left the hotel. As he waited on the pavement outside, a taxi arrived and a man got out. He began walking very slowly up the steps of the hotel. It was Eddie Stratton and he was very drunk. The taxi driver got out too and helped Eddie up the steps. Morse knew that the American was too drunk to answer any questions that night. But perhaps he could get some information from the taxi driver. He stopped the man as he came down the steps and he showed him his police identity card[35].

'Where did you pick that man up?' Morse asked him.

'From an address in North Oxford,' replied the driver. 'It was number ninety-seven, Hamilton Road. A woman phoned. She asked me to collect him and bring him to the Randolph Hotel. The woman's name was Mrs Williams.'

Morse was very surprised. Why had Eddie Stratton been at Sheila Williams's house?

————

Morse went quickly to the Police Headquarters. Sergeant Lewis was there. When he showed Morse the yellow tour programme, the inspector was very interested.

Next, Morse and Lewis drove together to Cherwell Lodge.

'You have a difficult job to do, Lewis,' Morse told the sergeant. 'You have to tell Marion Kemp about her husband's death. I'm going to visit Sheila Williams. She may have something very important to tell me. We know that Eddie Stratton was with her this evening.'

Lewis watched Morse walk in the direction of Hamilton Road. Then he rang the bell of the Kemps' flat.

'It's Sergeant Lewis from the Thames Valley Police, Mrs Kemp!' he called.

'All right, all right!' a woman's voice said crossly, inside the flat. A few minutes later Marion Kemp unlocked the door. Lewis looked down in surprise. Mrs Kemp was sitting in a wheelchair. She held a walking stick[36] across her knees.

'Didn't anybody tell you that I can't walk?' asked Marion. 'I can't move very far without a wheelchair.'

She turned the chair and wheeled herself into the sitting-room. Then she asked, 'Have you found my husband yet?'

'I have something to tell you —' began Lewis.

'Please sit down, Sergeant,' said Marion. 'I phoned the police because I need a little help. I can't put myself to bed – my husband always helps me.'

'Yes, I see,' said Lewis. He felt very sorry for Marion. He phoned the Police Headquarters and asked for a policewoman to come and help her.

'Thank you,' she said. 'You see, two years ago my husband crashed our car into another car. *He* wasn't hurt, but this is what he did to *me*.' Suddenly her voice was angry and full of hate.

'At what time did your husband leave this morning?' asked Lewis.

'At twenty past seven. A taxi came for him – my husband wasn't allowed to drive after he killed me.'

'He didn't *kill* you, madam,' said Lewis.

'Yes, he did!' she shouted. 'He killed the other woman and he killed me too!'

Lewis felt very uncomfortable. He did not want to listen to Marion Kemp saying these things.

'Did you know where he was going in London?' he asked.

'He went to his publishers. He's writing a book and they wanted to discuss it with him. He called me from their office.'

'And you don't know where he went when he got back to Oxford?'

'No. But perhaps he went to see his girlfriend – that dreadful Sheila Williams.'

'Mrs Kemp, I've got some bad news —' began Lewis.

At that moment, the door bell rang. Lewis stood up.

'That must be the policewoman. I'll just go and let her in.'

But Marion was staring at Lewis.

'He's dead. He's dead, Sergeant, isn't he?' she said very quietly.

'Yes, Mrs Kemp,' Lewis replied. 'He's dead.'

———

Morse was at Sheila Williams's house, drinking coffee. Sheila's house was pleasant and comfortable. Morse was a little surprised. The furniture was expensive and there were some interesting pictures on the wall. 'Sheila Williams has good taste[37],' thought Morse.

Morse had told her quietly about the death of Theodore Kemp. When he had finished, Sheila sat for a time in silence, her eyes filling with tears.

'But how — and why?' she said at last.

'We don't know. I thought that perhaps you could help us. What was your relationship with Dr Kemp, Mrs Williams?'

'He killed the other woman and he killed me too!'
Marion Kemp shouted.

'We'd been having an affair. He told me that he wanted to end it and we had an argument about that. But that wasn't a reason for him to kill himself.'

Sheila started to cry and Morse put his arms round her.

'I didn't say that he killed himself,' he said.

'How did he die then?' she asked.

'We can't be sure. But please be honest with me. Do you know anybody who wanted to kill Dr Kemp?'

'No,' said Sheila sadly. 'I don't know. But *I* didn't have anything to do with his death.'

'Where were you going at lunchtime?' asked Morse. 'Sergeant Lewis saw you walking in the direction of North Oxford.'

'I didn't go very far. I was going to a pub – to "The Bird and Baby",' replied Sheila slowly. Lots of University people used this name for the pub that was really called 'The Eagle and Child'. It was only two hundred metres from the Randolph Hotel.

'Were you on your own – in the pub?'

'Yes,' said Sheila. 'But I did see somebody cycling past, in the direction of North Oxford. It was Cedric – Cedric Downes.'

Suddenly, Sheila looked up at Morse, her eyes wide open. Morse knew that Sheila wanted him to stay. He wanted to stay, but he knew that he should leave immediately.

A few moments later, the inspector was walking back towards his car. Because he had left so quickly, he hadn't asked Sheila about Eddie Stratton's visit.

7

The Continental Seven

The next morning, Morse and Lewis met at 7.45. They were both very tired, but they had to discuss what they were going to do next.

The tourists had been going to leave Oxford that morning at 9.30. The next part of the tour was a visit to Stratford-upon-Avon. But now, after Kemp's death, Morse and Lewis would have to interview all the members of the group again. They would have to find out what everybody had been doing the previous afternoon.

Morse wanted to talk to Cedric Downes as soon as possible. Sheila Williams had seen Downes cycling away from the Randolph Hotel at lunchtime the previous day. Why had he left the hotel and where was he going?

A little later, as Morse and Lewis drove to the Randolph, Lewis asked a question.

'You haven't forgotten about Ashenden, have you, sir? We ought to talk to him. When Kemp phoned from London yesterday, it was Ashenden who took the call. And he did lie to us about looking round Magdalen College on Thursday.'

'No, Lewis, I haven't forgotten about Ashenden,' replied Morse. 'We'll talk to him. And we also have to find out which of the Americans left their tour programme in the University Parks yesterday afternoon.'

'Did you notice the number seven on that tour programme?' asked Lewis. 'It was written in a strange way – with a line through it.'

'Yes, you're right. That's the normal way of writing a seven in continental Europe[38],' said Morse. 'But it's unusual for an American to write a seven in that way. So this seven is an excellent piece of evidence for us. If we can find out which person in the group writes a continental seven, we'll know who the tour programme belonged to. We'll know who was at Parson's Pleasure.'

———

At 9.30 a.m., Morse and Lewis were sitting with John Ashenden, Sheila Williams and the manager of the Randolph Hotel, in the manager's office. The inspector explained that because of Kemp's murder, the tour could not leave Oxford until after lunch.

'When did these Americans arrive in Britain?' he asked Ashenden.

'On the 27th of October,' the tour leader replied.

Morse smiled. Ashenden stood up and left the room. He had a lot of arrangements to make. He had to cancel the group's lunch in Stratford. And he had to explain to the hotel there that the tour group would arrive late.

Then Morse turned to the hotel manager. 'I wonder if you can help me,' he said. 'I want to find out what everybody on the tour was doing yesterday afternoon. So I've prepared a short questionnaire[39]. Could your secretary please make a copy for each person in the group?'

Morse handed a piece of paper to the hotel manager.

(a) Name

(b) Home address

(c) Where were you between 3.00 and 6.30p.m. on Friday, 2nd November?

(d) Date of your arrival in Britain

Signature

'Yes, of course, Inspector,' the manager replied. He took Morse's questionnaire and went out of the room.

Then Morse turned to Sheila Williams.

'Perhaps you could arrange something for the group to do after the meeting,' he said. 'Could you give them a talk? Or perhaps they could just go for a walk round Oxford?'

'I don't mean to be difficult,' replied Sheila, 'but I'm not really the person who should do that. I don't know enough about the architecture of Oxford. But I think that Cedric Downes is free this morning. He could talk to them.'

'Good,' said Morse. 'Could you phone him?'

'I think that *you* should phone him, Inspector,' said Sheila. 'He probably doesn't know about Dr Kemp's death.'

'Unless *he* was the person who murdered him,' said Morse quietly.

———

When Morse called Cedric Downes's number, Downes's wife, Lucy, answered. Her voice was very soft and she sounded a little sad.

'How can I help you?' she asked.

'Mrs Downes? It's Chief Inspector Morse here. Is your husband at home?'

After a minute, Morse heard Downes pick up the phone.

'Inspector? Cedric Downes here. Can I help?'

'Certainly, sir. I'm speaking from the Randolph Hotel. I have some sad news.'

'Yes, I know,' said Downes. 'Theo's dead. Ashenden phoned me earlier.'

Morse was not very pleased that Ashenden had told Downes about Kemp's death. But he only said, 'We're very busy this morning. Could you help us? Could you come and take the tour group for a walk round Oxford?'

'Yes, of course,' said Downes. 'And I could take them to

the Ashmolean Museum.'

'That's splendid!' said Morse. 'Thank you very much. By the way, I want to ask you some questions about yesterday afternoon. Somebody saw you cycling towards North Oxford at about lunchtime. Where were you going?'

'My hearing-aid wasn't working properly yesterday morning,' replied Downes. 'So I went home at lunchtime to get my spare one.'

'I see,' said Morse. 'But your hearing isn't *very* bad, is it, sir? You don't seem to have any problems hearing me now.'

'That's because my dear wife gave me a special phone attachment[40] for my birthday,' Downes said. 'If I use this attachment, I can hear everything clearly.'

'You're very happy with your wife, aren't you, sir?' asked Morse.

'Yes. I love her more than anything in the world,' replied Downes. 'I would do *anything* to keep her with me.'

'*Anything* – including murder?' asked Morse suddenly.

'Oh, yes, Inspector,' said Downes quietly. Then he continued, 'I know that Sheila was the person who saw me yesterday afternoon. I saw her too. And I also saw another person from the group walking towards North Oxford. It was John Ashenden.'

———

Ashenden had called the tour group together. Morse told them about Kemp's death and said that because of this, the tour could not leave Oxford until the evening. Then he gave each of them a copy of his questionnaire.

'We have to ask everybody on the tour some questions about yesterday afternoon,' Morse went on. 'So I've prepared a short questionnaire for each of you to fill in. When you've done that, Mr Downes is going to lead you on a walk round Oxford.

'Please try to remember as much as you can about yester-day. Your information is very important. A theft and two deaths have happened here. A jewel has been stolen and Mrs Stratton, the person who brought it to Oxford, has died. And now Dr Kemp, the person who was going to receive it, has been murdered.'

Ten minutes later, everyone in the group had filled in their questionnaire. As soon as the tourists had gone out with Cedric Downes, Morse and Lewis looked quickly through the papers. Morse felt very pleased. He saw at once that only one person had used a continental seven on his questionnaire.

On Howard Brown's questionnaire, beside question *(d)*, Brown had written,

(d) Date of your arrival in Britain _ 27 October ____

'So it was Howard Brown's tour programme in the University Parks,' said Morse. 'That's very interesting. When was Howard Brown in the Parks and what was he doing there?'

Morse was particularly interested in two other people from the group. Eddie Stratton was one. Stratton was still in bed with a bad headache from the alcohol he had drunk the previous evening. 'Where was he yesterday afternoon?' wondered Morse.

And then there was John Ashenden. Downes had said that he had passed Ashenden walking towards North Oxford yesterday. So where had Ashenden been going? And why had he lied about visiting Magdalen College the day before?

8

Questions and Answers

Later that morning, Morse went to see Max at the mortuary[41] where he worked. Max showed him Theodore Kemp's body.

'There are some bruises here,' said Max, pointing to some dark marks on Kemp's forehead. Then he turned the head and Morse saw a terrible wound in the back of Kemp's skull[42]. Morse felt sick as he looked at it. Max covered the body with a sheet.

'What did kill him?' asked Morse. 'The injuries to the front of his head, or the wound at the back of his skull?'

'Probably the wound at the back,' replied Max. 'Perhaps somebody hit him on the front of his head and he fell over.' The pathologist pointed to Morse's skull as he spoke. 'Perhaps as he fell, he hit the back of his head on something hard.'

'Do you think that he was naked when he was murdered?'

'I don't know,' replied Max. 'Perhaps.'

'But *why* was he naked?' Morse asked himself. 'What was he doing? Was he making love with a woman?'

———

Eddie Stratton was still in his room suffering from a bad headache. But he could not rest. He was thinking about his first meeting with his wife, Laura.

In California, Stratton worked as a mortician[43]. He arranged people's funerals when they died, and prepared their dead bodies for their funerals. He made bodies look peaceful, to please the family and friends of the people who had died. Sometimes this was difficult, especially if the person had died in an accident. But Stratton was very good at his job.

Eddie had met his wife Laura when her first husband, Cyrus, had died. He had prepared Cyrus's body for his funeral.

'Perhaps somebody hit him on the front of his head and he fell over,' replied Max.

Then a year later, he had married Laura. Laura was lonely after Cyrus's death and needed a new husband.

Eddie started thinking about the Wolvercote Tongue. It was insured for a lot of money, and if it was lost or stolen the insurance company would have to pay. But would the money go to him, or would it go to the Ashmolean Museum? Cyrus Palmer had left the jewel to the museum, not to Laura. So did the museum own it already?

There was a knock at the door and Morse and Lewis came into the room.

'Good morning, sir,' said Morse. 'We have to ask you a few questions. Can you tell us where you went yesterday afternoon?'

Stratton was ready to answer Morse's questions. He said that he had seen an article in the local newspaper, *The Oxford Mail*, at lunchtime the previous day. The article was about an exhibition of old railway engines at the Railway Centre in Didcot, a small town near Oxford. Stratton said that he was very interested in old trains, so he had gone to Didcot and spent the afternoon there. He had returned to Oxford just after five o'clock.

When he arrived at Oxford Station, he'd had a drink in the bar there. Then he'd gone to a restaurant and he'd eaten a meal by himself. On his way back to the hotel, he'd met Sheila Williams. They had talked for a few minutes and she'd invited him back to her house for a drink. He had drunk a lot of whisky. At the end of the evening, Sheila had called for a taxi to take him back to the Randolph.

Morse liked Eddie Stratton's honest face and his simple, quiet way of talking. He thought that the man was telling the truth. But then Lewis spoke.

'I'm sorry, sir, but you can't be telling the truth. You couldn't have had a drink in Oxford Station yesterday. The bar was closed all day for repairs.'

Suddenly, Stratton looked very uncomfortable. For a few moments he said nothing. Then at last he spoke.

'You're quite right, Sergeant. I didn't have a drink at the station. But I did stay there for about half an hour after I got off the train. I didn't want to go out of the station immediately. I didn't want to meet anybody from the group while I was waiting for a taxi.'

'Do you mean that you'd seen somebody you knew on the train?' asked Morse. 'When you got on the train at Didcot, was that person already on the train?'

'Yes,' said Stratton. 'He didn't get on the train at Didcot.'

'The train had started from London,' said Morse. 'Perhaps the person got on the train there, or at Reading.' He looked across at Lewis. 'Kemp had telephoned the Randolph from London,' Morse was thinking. 'Did Stratton see Kemp on the train?'

'Tell me the name of the person you saw,' said Morse.

'It was Phil Aldrich,' replied Stratton quietly.

Morse was very surprised. He had not expected this answer. What was Phil Aldrich doing on the train? He said, 'I have one more question, sir. Are you hoping to get a lot of money from your wife's insurance company, now that she's dead?'

'Yes,' said Stratton. 'I'll be honest with you, Inspector. I'm not a rich man, and I'll be very happy to get the money from the insurance company.'

———

A few minutes later, Morse had found a London–Oxford train timetable at the hotel reception desk. Now he and Lewis were studying it in the manager's office.

'We have to find out what time Kemp left London,' said Morse. 'There was a train which left Paddington Station[44] at one thirty and arrived in Oxford at two fifty-seven. Was Kemp on that train? Eddie Stratton told us that *he* caught a train from Didcot to Oxford at just after five o'clock. That must have been the four twenty from London which stops at Didcot at five ten. It arrives in Oxford at five twenty-nine. If Kemp was on *that* train, Stratton didn't see him.'

'I've been wondering about that phone call,' said Lewis. 'The call that Kemp made to the Randolph Hotel at about twelve thirty.'

'Ashenden took that call,' said Morse. 'We have to find out more details from him. We need to know exactly what Kemp said. Yes, we must talk to Ashenden at once. Go and find him, Lewis.'

When Lewis brought Ashenden into the room, Morse asked the tour leader to remember his conversation with Dr Kemp, and to write it down on a piece of paper. Ten minutes later, Ashenden handed the paper to Morse.

Kemp: I've been delayed at Paddington, John.

Ashenden: Oh. What's the problem, Dr Kemp?

Kemp: I've missed the half-past twelve train. I'll take the train at half-past one. I'll be with you at quarter-past three. I'm sorry to miss lunch with the tour group.

Ashenden: Don't worry about it. I'll explain that you've been delayed. Shall I arrange for a taxi to meet you at the station?

Kemp: Yes, that's a good idea. My train arrives at Oxford just before three o'clock.

Ashenden: OK, I'll call a taxi company and ask someone to meet you at three o'clock.

Kemp: Thank you, John. Goodbye. I'll see you later.

'Did any of the other people in the group hear you speaking on the phone?' asked Morse.

'Perhaps,' replied Ashenden. 'Mrs Roscoe was sitting near me when the call came through. She has very good hearing.'

When Ashenden had gone, Morse said, 'Somebody phoned the hotel – we know that – but perhaps it wasn't Kemp. Ashenden could be lying. Perhaps it was somebody else who phoned. Perhaps Kemp was already dead!'

'Let's ask the receptionist about the call,' said Lewis. 'She put it through it to Ashenden. She heard the caller's voice too.'

The receptionist remembered the call very clearly. She was sure that the call was from Kemp because she knew his voice very well. Before she'd got her job at the Randolph, she had worked at the Ashmolean Museum and she'd spoken to Kemp on the phone many times.

Morse was disappointed. His idea about somebody else making the call had been wrong.

'Well, what about Howard Brown?' asked Lewis. 'The man who writes the continental seven? Shall I go and find him?'

'Not yet,' replied Morse. 'He's walking round Oxford with Cedric Downes. Let's go and see somebody else. What's Mr Downes's address? I'd like to talk to his wife, Lucy.'

When Morse rang the doorbell of Cedric Downes's house in Lonsdale Road, Lucy answered it at once. She was a very attractive woman in her early thirties. She had pretty blonde hair. When Morse and Lewis showed her their police identity cards, she smiled warmly.

'Is Mr Downes in?' asked Lewis.

'He's not here,' Lucy replied. 'He's taking some Americans on a tour round Oxford this morning. Can I help?'

'May we come in?' asked Morse.

'Yes, of course,' said Lucy. 'But I'm just on my way to London. A taxi will arrive very soon to take me to the railway station.'

As Morse entered the hallway of the house, he hit his leg against a large suitcase standing just inside the door.

'I'm so sorry, Inspector,' said Lucy. 'The case is by the door because I'm going to take it to London. There are curtains inside. A shop in London made them for me, but they made a mistake about the size. So I've got to take them back to the shop. They've made some new ones, which I'll collect at the same time.'

'I see,' said Morse. 'Well, we won't delay you for long, madam. We just have a few questions about yesterday.'

'Of course!' said Lucy. 'It's awful, isn't it, about poor Theo's death.'

'Mrs Downes, did your husband come back home at lunchtime yesterday?'

'Yes,' replied Lucy. 'Cedric came home to get his spare hearing-aid. He said that his other one wasn't working properly and that he wanted to change it.'

Just then somebody rang the doorbell.

'There's the taxi driver,' said Lucy. 'Shall I ask him to wait?'

'No, that's all I wanted to ask you,' Morse said.

Lewis picked up the heavy suitcase and carried it out to the taxi. Lucy smiled warmly at him.

'When are you coming back, Mrs Downes?' asked Morse.

'At seven o'clock. Cedric is coming to meet me at the station.'

She climbed into the taxi. The two policemen stood and watched as the taxi drove away down Lonsdale Road.

'What a lovely woman!' said Lewis.

Morse did not reply for a minute. Then he said, 'Lewis, something is worrying me. I know that there's a connection between the theft of the Wolvercote Tongue and the murder of Theodore Kemp. I don't know what this link is. But I think that your "lovely woman" might know something about it!'

9

Secrets from the Past

On the way back to the Randolph Hotel, Morse decided to visit the University Parks again. He wanted to see in the daylight the place where Kemp's body had been found.

When they arrived at Parson's Pleasure, Sergeant Dixon was there already. Sergeant Dixon worked for the Thames Valley Police too, and he was helping Morse and Lewis to investigate the murder. He told them that nothing connected with Kemp had been found in the cubicles. And none of Kemp's clothes had been found anywhere.

'I don't think that Kemp had been swimming in the river when he died,' said Lewis. 'The water is too cold at this time of year.'

'So why did somebody put his body in the river?' said Morse. 'And why was he naked? Was he making love with a woman before he died? Perhaps he was making love with Sheila Williams?'

'Do you think that Mrs Williams killed Kemp, sir?' asked Lewis.

'Well, she had a strong motive[45] to kill Kemp,' Morse

'I don't think that Kemp had been swimming in the river when he died,' said Lewis. 'The water is too cold at this time of year.'

said. 'She was angry and upset because he'd ended their affair. But I don't think that *she* put his body in the river. It would have been too heavy for her to lift.'

While Lewis talked with Sergeant Dixon for a few minutes, Morse went to sit in the police car. There was a map of Oxford in the car. Morse opened it and found the River Cherwell. He moved his finger along the thin blue line of the river, from where it joined the River Thames. His finger followed the Cherwell through Oxford. It followed the river northwards from the University Parks, then up past the gardens of the houses in Lonsdale Road, and Hamilton Road.

It had rained earlier in the week and the river had been very full for several days. 'A lot of water has come down through the University Parks,' thought Morse. 'If something was put into the water at a place further up the river, the water would have carried it quickly down to the Parks. If a body was put into the river at Lonsdale Road, for example —'

The Downes' house was in Lonsdale Road and their garden sloped down to the banks of the River Cherwell. Had Kemp been murdered at the Downes' house and his body put into the river there?

'Lewis loves his wife very much, and he isn't interested in other women. But even *he* noticed that Downes's wife, Lucy, is very attractive,' thought Morse. 'Theodore Kemp liked women very much, and his own wife is not well. Did Kemp lose interest in Sheila Williams because he'd started an affair with Lucy Downes? And did Cedric Downes find out about the affair and murder him?'

Lewis got back into the car. He saw Morse's finger on the map, pointing to Lonsdale Road.

'I know what you're thinking, sir,' he said. 'But Cedric Downes couldn't have murdered Kemp. He has a very good alibi – he can prove that he was in another place at the time of the murder. He was with the American group all afternoon yesterday.'

'But perhaps it was *Lucy* Downes who murdered Kemp,' said Morse.

Lewis was shocked. 'You can't think that, sir!' he said.

'I can think anything I want to, Lewis!' Morse replied. 'But we have to go back to the Randolph Hotel now. We can't keep the Americans in Oxford all day. And we have some more questions to ask Phil Aldrich and Howard Brown about what they were doing yesterday afternoon.'

———

Sheila Williams was at the Randolph, having lunch with the group. Most of the Americans wanted to leave Oxford and go on to Stratford-upon-Avon. But Morse had said that the tour could not leave until six o'clock. Mrs Janet Roscoe was behaving in a very difficult way. She complained loudly about the delay.

Only Phil Aldrich seemed as quiet and patient as usual. He had not complained when Morse and Lewis had arrived at the hotel and interrupted him in the middle of his lunch. Morse had taken him to another room and had asked him to write a statement about his movements the previous afternoon.

Sheila Williams stood in the doorway of the room and watched Aldrich writing. He wrote very quickly and easily. He stopped only once, when Janet Roscoe came into the room and started complaining about the tour. Usually Aldrich listened to Janet patiently, but now he spoke to her in a loud and angry voice.

'I haven't time to listen to you now, Janet,' he said. 'Please go away and leave me alone.'

Sheila was very surprised about the angry way in which

Phil Aldrich spoke. Several other members of the group had heard it too. Janet Roscoe left the room at once. She looked shocked and unhappy.

Sergeant Lewis was also watching Aldrich. Like Sheila, he was surprised at how easily Aldrich wrote his statement. When Aldrich handed the statement to Lewis, the sergeant read it quickly.

Then he took the statement to Morse. 'This is interesting, sir,' he said. 'Mr Aldrich was stationed[46] in Oxford during the Second World War.'

Morse read the statement slowly and carefully.

During the Second World War, I was a soldier in the US Army. In early 1944, I was stationed in Oxford. There I met a married woman whose husband was away at sea. I fell in love with her and we had an affair. On 2nd January 1945, she had a baby. This baby was my daughter. We gave her the name Philippa, because my own name is Philip. We always called her 'Pippa'.

When the war finished, I went back to the States and the woman's husband came home. He looked after my Pippa as if she was his own daughter.

But in 1962, Pippa ran away from home. Her mother wrote to tell me that Pippa was living among homeless people in the King's Cross[47] area of London.

Pippa's mother died last year – her husband had already died in 1986. So I decided to come to England, to try to find Pippa. I have no other children, so finding her was very important to me.

I saw an advertisement for this tour in a California newspaper. I noticed that the tour would stay in London for three days, so I joined the tour. When I arrived in London, I went to all the places for homeless people in the King's Cross area. On the third day, I spoke to a man who knew my daughter. He said that he had seen her the previous week. But the tour was going to leave

London that day, so I gave the man the phone numbers of the hotels where we were going to stay. I asked him to find Pippa and give the phone numbers to her.

Yesterday, Pippa called me in my room at the Randolph. She asked me to meet her at Paddington Station at 2.15 in the afternoon. I took a train to London at once and I arrived there just after 2 p.m. I waited at the station for over two hours, but Pippa didn't come. So I took the 4.20 train back to Oxford.

I didn't see Eddie Stratton when he got on the train at Didcot Station. But now I know that he saw me, because he told me this morning.

Philip Aldrich

As Morse read through Aldrich's statement, Lewis watched him carefully. When Morse had finished reading, he said, 'Well, Lewis? What do you think about this statement?'

'It's very sad about his daughter,' replied Lewis. 'Why didn't she meet him at the station?'

'I don't know,' said Morse. 'But I'm not sure that I believe Mr Aldrich completely. He isn't telling us the whole truth.

'I think that he *did* go to London yesterday, but I'm not sure about *why* he went there. And I'm not sure about what *Kemp* was doing after he left his publishers. Perhaps Kemp and Aldrich met each other in London.'

Lewis shook his head. He did not think that Morse was right.

'There's another thing, Lewis,' Morse went on. 'Phil Aldrich, Eddie Stratton and Howard Brown are all about the same age. Were they all soldiers in the US Army? Were they all stationed in Oxford during the Second World War? Perhaps the other two also have secrets from the past. Perhaps they *all* had love affairs during the war!'

Next, Morse interviewed Howard Brown and showed him the tour programme with the continental seven. He said that it had been found in the University Parks. At once, Brown agreed that it was his programme. He also said that he had gone to the University Parks the previous day.

Then Brown told Morse that he *had* been stationed in Oxford in 1944. And Eddie Stratton had been stationed in Oxford at that time too. They had known each other during the war, and they had been very pleased to meet each other again. They had enjoyed talking about their time in the army.

'When I was in Oxford in 1944,' Brown told Morse, 'I fell in love. I fell in love with a British woman called Betty Fowler. But after the war, I went back to America. Later, I went to live in California and there, I married Shirley. I wrote to Betty telling her the news and giving her my address.

'For many years I didn't hear from Betty,' Brown went on. 'But six months ago, I received a letter from her. She wrote to say that she had been married too, but that her husband had died. She gave me her phone number and said that if I ever came to Britain, she would love to see me again.

'When I saw an advertisement for the tour, I wanted to come to England and meet Betty again. So when we arrived here in Oxford, and my wife went out for a walk with Eddie Stratton, I stayed in the hotel and I called Betty. We arranged to meet in the University Parks yesterday afternoon. We talked a lot about old times, and we kissed a little. I must have dropped my tour programme then.'

'I see, Mr Brown,' said Morse. 'Well, thank you for being honest with me.'

Howard Brown stood up to go, but then he spoke again.

'There's one more thing, Inspector. When I was walking to the Parks yesterday afternoon, I saw somebody from the group standing at the bus-stop outside St Giles' Church. I think that he was waiting for a bus to go towards Summertown[48].'

'And who was that, sir?' asked Morse.

'It was Mr Ashenden,' replied Brown.

When Howard Brown had gone, Lewis said, 'Well, what did you think, sir? *I* think that he was telling us the truth.'

'Yes, I agree, Lewis,' replied Morse. 'But *somebody* isn't telling us the truth. Somebody stole the Wolvercote Tongue and somebody murdered Theodore Kemp. I wish that I could see the connection!'

10

Ashenden's Bet

Both Cedric Downes and Howard Brown had told Morse that they had seen John Ashenden going towards North Oxford on the previous afternoon. So Morse decided that it was time to ask Ashenden some questions.

'First, why did you lie to me about visiting Magdalen College on the day you arrived here?' Morse asked him. 'We know that the college was closed on that day.'

Ashenden did not seem very surprised by Morse's question.

'It wasn't really a lie,' he replied. 'I did go to Magdalen, but I found that the college was closed. So I walked back into the city centre.'

'And what were you doing yesterday afternoon, when you

were seen going towards North Oxford?'

'I was on my way to Summertown,' replied Ashenden. 'I spent the afternoon in a betting shop[49] there. There was a big race at three fifteen, so I bet five pounds on one of the horses. The horse was called 'Thetford Queen'. It didn't win the race.'

'Would anybody at the betting shop remember you?' asked Lewis.

'I don't know,' replied Ashenden. 'It was very busy and a lot of people came into the shop. But I can prove that I was there.' He took a black leather wallet from the pocket of his jacket and opened it. There was a small piece of pink paper inside.

'This is my betting-slip,' said Ashenden. 'It shows that I put five pounds on Thetford Queen, and it shows the time that I made the bet – it was about two thirty.'

He handed the betting-slip to the inspector.

'Thank you, sir,' said Morse. 'I'll keep this. You're free to go now. And the group can leave at five o'clock, not six. It isn't far to Stratford-upon-Avon.'

———

Soon after five o'clock the tour coach was leaving the hotel, travelling north on its way to Stratford.

Ashenden was sitting in his usual seat at the front of the coach. On the opposite side of the coach, in the seat immediately behind the driver, sat Mrs Janet Roscoe. She was reading one of Shakespeare's plays, and she did not look up from her book. But she did not seem happy. Behind Ashenden were Howard and Shirley Brown. They too were silent.

As usual, Phil Aldrich was sitting right at the back of the coach. Everybody in the group had noticed the sudden coolness[50] which had grown between him and Janet Roscoe

Soon after five o'clock, the tour coach was travelling north on its way to Stratford.

after he had spoken angrily to her at the hotel.

Two people from the group which had arrived in Oxford two days ago, were not on the coach. The dead body of Mrs Laura Stratton was lying in the mortuary in Oxford. Eddie Stratton was on his way to London. He had left the tour and had made arrangements for Laura's body to be taken back to California.

Ashenden was thinking about Chief Inspector Morse. Many people had told him that Morse was very clever. Should he be worried?

'Is everything going to be all right?' he thought.

———

From a window of the Randolph Hotel, Morse and Lewis watched the coach drive away.

'Will we be seeing that group again, sir?' asked Lewis.

'No,' said Morse. He sounded bored.

'Does that mean that you know who stole the jewel and who murdered Kemp?' asked Lewis.

'No,' said Morse. 'We've had lots of evidence in this case, haven't we, Lewis? There are many things which could help us to solve the crimes. But I've a feeling that we've missed the really important evidence.'

'Should we go to see Mrs Kemp, sir?' asked Lewis. But Morse was not listening.

'I think that Kemp was murdered because he was having an affair,' Morse said quietly. 'But I don't think that it was his affair with Sheila Williams. It was —'

Suddenly Morse stopped. He had bought a copy of *The Times* newspaper on his way to the Randolph that morning. Now he looked again at the pink betting-slip which Ashenden had given him. He looked at the horse's name on it – Thetford Queen. Then he turned to the sports pages of the newspaper and found the results of the previous day's horse races.

67

'Look, Lewis!' he said. His eyes were wide with surprise. 'Thetford Queen, the horse that Ashenden bet on, came first in its race. The odds were thirty-to-one, so nobody really expected the horse to win. Ashenden bet five pounds on that horse. So he has won a lot of money – he has won one hundred and fifty pounds. But *he* told us that the horse didn't win.'

'And he didn't collect the money he'd won, sir,' said Lewis. 'When you collect your money, you have to hand in your betting-slip. But Ashenden kept his betting-slip. That's very strange.'

'Why didn't he collect his money?' said Morse. 'Because he was no longer in the betting shop, Lewis!

'Ashenden went to that betting shop to give himself an alibi. He wanted us to think that he was there all afternoon. He put the bet on the horse at two thirty, but then he left. He didn't expect the horse to win the race!'

'But where did he go when he left the betting shop?' asked Lewis.

'Perhaps he went to Oxford Station and met Theodore Kemp's train at three o'clock,' Morse replied. 'Perhaps he went somewhere with Kemp.'

At that moment, the manager of the Randolph Hotel hurried in. 'There's a phone call for you, Inspector,' he said. 'It's very urgent.'

Morse went to the phone. It was Max, the pathologist.

'Morse?' he said. 'I'm at the Kemps' flat. Can you come here at once? Marion Kemp has tried to kill herself.'

———

When Morse and Lewis arrived at the flat, Marion had already been taken to the Radcliffe Infirmary, the main hospital in Oxford. On a small table beside her bed stood an empty bottle that had contained sleeping pills. Beside the bottle there was a note.

IF I'M STILL ALIVE WHEN
YOU FIND ME, PLEASE LET
ME DIE.

There was a garden all round the block of flats where the Kemps lived, and Morse had seen a young gardener working in the front part of it, near the road. Beside him there was a wheelbarrow[51] for carrying things away.

Morse had found a photograph of Theodore Kemp in the Kemps' sitting-room. He took it outside and showed it to the young gardener.

'Have you seen this man before?' he asked.

'Yes,' replied the gardener. 'He lives here.'

'Did you see him going into the flats yesterday afternoon?'

'I don't remember seeing him,' said the gardener. 'But I was working in the back part of the garden most of yesterday afternoon.'

Morse and Lewis walked round to the back of the block of flats. There was an area of grass that sloped down to the River Cherwell. The water was flowing strong and fast. It was carrying lots of dead branches from trees.

'It could easily carry a body too, all the way down to the University Parks,' Morse thought.

Morse stared at the river as a new idea started to grow in his mind. 'Let's go to a pub for a drink, Lewis,' he said. Sometimes when he drank beer, Morse could think better.

———

'Why do you think Mrs Kemp tried to kill herself, sir?' asked Lewis, when they were sitting in the pub.

'I don't know,' replied Morse. 'Perhaps she loved her husband so much that she couldn't live without him.'

Lewis thought about Marion Kemp. He had spoken to

her the previous evening. Then, she had seemed full of hate for her husband. But when he had told her about Kemp's death, she had been very upset. It was difficult to know how she really felt about Kemp. She hated him because of what he had done to her in the car accident, but perhaps she loved him too.

'Give me some new ideas, Lewis,' Morse was saying. 'I still have to find the connection between the theft of the jewel and Kemp's murder.'

'I'm tired, sir,' said Lewis. 'I can't think of any new ideas.'

'Then go home and rest,' said Morse crossly. 'I can ask Sergeant Dixon to come and help me instead.'

'But I don't want to go home,' said Lewis. 'My wife's decorating the house and everything's in a mess. She's putting new wallpaper on all the walls. And now she says that we need new curtains.'

'That's it!' shouted Morse. 'Curtains!' He jumped up, very excited. 'You've done it again, my old friend!'

Lewis got up too, a puzzled expression on his face. What had he said? He didn't understand why Morse was so excited about curtains. Sometimes he didn't understand Morse at all.

11

Morse Makes an Arrest

At six fifteen that evening, Morse went to visit Sheila Williams. Lewis waited for him in the police car, outside Sheila's house.

'I'm very sorry to tell you this,' Morse said to Sheila, 'but

Mrs Kemp tried to kill herself this afternoon. She's in the Radcliffe Infirmary now.'

Sheila put her hand over her mouth. She was very shocked and upset.

'No!' she said and she began to cry. Then suddenly she put her head on Morse's shoulder and held him tightly.

'Did she love her husband?' asked Morse gently.

Sheila pulled away from him. 'No,' she answered in an angry voice. '*I* was the only woman who really loved Theo.'

'Do you know anybody else who was close to him? Was there a third woman in his life? Please tell me the truth, Sheila.'

'He always said that there wasn't anybody else,' Sheila replied quietly. 'But —'

'I think that you know who it was,' Morse went on. 'Don't you, Sheila?'

Sheila nodded miserably.

'It was Lucy Downes, wasn't it?' said Morse. 'But his affair with her only started a short time ago. Am I right?'

———

Lewis was waiting in the car. The door of the house opened. The sergeant could see that Sheila was upset – she was crying as she said goodbye to Morse. The inspector came slowly back to the car.

'Curtains!' said Morse. 'As you said, Lewis – curtains.'

'But why are curtains important, sir?' asked Lewis.

'Mrs Downes took a suitcase to London this morning,' said Morse. 'She said that it contained curtains which she was going to take back to a shop there. But she wasn't telling the truth. There were no curtains inside the case.'

'Then what was in the suitcase, sir?' asked Lewis.

'Theodore Kemp's clothes!' said Morse. 'Cedric Downes murdered Kemp and afterwards, he put the dead man's clothes in a suitcase. He told his wife to take the suitcase to London and to get rid of it[52].'

Morse told Lewis to drive to the Downes' house. When they arrived, all the windows of the house were dark. Morse looked at his watch. It was just after half-past six.

'Downes isn't here,' he said. 'He's gone to the station to meet his wife from the seven o'clock train from London. Let's have a look around.'

Morse and Lewis walked round the house and into the Downes' back garden. The garden sloped down to the River Cherwell. Lewis shone his torch, and by its light, they saw a path leading to the edge of the water.

'*This* was the place,' said Morse. 'This was where Downes put Theodore Kemp's body into the river.

'I think this is what happened, Lewis,' Morse went on. 'Kemp had become tired of Sheila Williams and he'd started an affair with Lucy Downes. But Cedric Downes found out about the affair and so he killed Kemp. Then he had to get rid of Kemp's body, so he carried it down to the river and he put it into the water. The river carried the body down to the University Parks.'

Morse and Lewis went back to the car. Suddenly they heard a voice on the car radio. It was Sergeant Dixon at St Aldate's Police Station.

'I'm afraid there's bad news,' he said. 'Mrs Kemp has died at the hospital.'

Morse stared up at the sky with a tired face. He felt very sad about Marion Kemp's death. The woman had had an unhappy life, and now she had killed herself.

'Come on, Lewis,' he said suddenly. 'We've got seven minutes to get to the station. I want to be there when Mrs Downes's train arrives!'

———

When Morse and Lewis arrived at Oxford station, the train from London had just arrived. Morse and Lewis got out of their car and ran onto the platform.

The train was standing at the platform. Cedric Downes was walking from one carriage to another and looking in all the windows. Morse and Lewis followed him as he walked along the train. As Downes looked inside the last carriage, the train began to move slowly out of the station.

Downes turned and walked back down the platform. Lewis stepped out in front of him.

'Good evening, sir.'

Downes was surprised to see Lewis. 'Hello, Sergeant. Do you want to ask me some more questions about Theo Kemp?' he asked. 'I'm sorry, but I've nothing more to tell you.'

Then Morse appeared beside Lewis.

'Were you hoping to meet your wife, Mr Downes?' he asked.

'What? Just a minute, Inspector.' Downes put his hand in his pocket and took out his hearing-aid. He put it in his right ear but it made some high whistling noises. 'I'm sorry, there's something wrong with this hearing-aid. I'll have to go back to my car and get my spare one.'

'We'll walk to your car with you,' said Morse.

In front of the railway station a second police car was waiting, with two policemen inside it. Morse had called St Aldate's Police Station and asked for two more officers to be sent to the railway station.

Downes walked out of the station to the parking area where he had left his car. He unlocked the car, found his other hearing-aid, and put it in his ear.

'That's better, I can hear you now,' said Downes. 'You were trying to tell me something, Inspector?'

'No,' said Morse. 'I'm not *trying* to tell you something – I *am* telling you something. We'd like you to come with us, sir. Please give me your car keys.'

'What's all this about, Inspector?' asked Downes angrily.

'Your keys, please, Mr Downes,' Morse said calmly.

Downes handed his keys to Morse. Then Morse called over the two policemen from the other car. When they were standing on either side of Downes, the inspector spoke again.

'Cedric Downes, I arrest[53] you on suspicion of the murder of Dr Theodore Kemp.'

Downes stared at Morse with his mouth open. He did not move or say anything.

———

After Downes had been driven away in the other police car, Lewis asked Morse a question.

'Are you *sure* that Downes killed Theodore Kemp, sir?'

'Oh, yes,' said Morse.

'Please explain to me what happened,' said Lewis.

'Dr Kemp made a phone call to the Randolph Hotel at about twelve thirty yesterday afternoon,' said Morse. 'He said that he was in London – he wanted people to think that he was in London. But he didn't make that call from London – he made it from Oxford.'

'Ashenden took the call and Kemp told him that he was in London. He said that he had missed his train and would be late. So Ashenden told Sheila Williams and Downes, and the rest of the group, that Kemp was still in London and would not be back until three o'clock.

'After he'd made the phone call, Kemp went at once to the Downes' house,' Morse went on. 'He went there to make love to his new girlfriend, Lucy Downes. But unfortunately for him, things went wrong. Cedric Downes came home unexpectedly to get a spare hearing-aid. He found his wife upstairs in bed with Kemp, and he was very angry. When

'Cedric Downes, I arrest you on suspicion of the murder
of Dr Theodore Kemp.'

Kemp got up from the bed, Downes hit him over the head with something heavy – perhaps a walking stick. Kemp fell, hit his head on something sharp – perhaps the corner of the fireplace – and died.

'Downes had no time to get rid of Kemp's naked body, because he had to get back to the tour group. So he told his wife to pack Kemp's clothes in a suitcase, and to clean up all the blood.

'The River Cherwell runs at the bottom of the garden of the Downes' house. That evening, Downes carried Kemp's body down the stairs, put it in a wheelbarrow and wheeled it across the grass to the river. It was quite dark then, and it was easy for him to push the body into the Cherwell without being seen.

'Two hours later, the body had been carried by the river to the University Parks, where it was seen by the two young lovers at Parson's Pleasure.'

When Morse had finished speaking, Lewis said, 'So Downes was the murderer. And Eddie Stratton, Howard Brown and Phil Aldrich had nothing to do with Kemp's death?'

'That's right! But Kemp's murder is only half the case,' replied Morse. 'We still have to find out what happened to the Wolvercote Tongue.'

––––––

By 6.30 that evening, the American tourists had arrived at the Swan Hotel in Stratford-upon-Avon, where they were going to stay. Dinner was not until 8.30, so the group had some free time. John Ashenden left his room. He went down to the lounge of the hotel, where some members of the group were sitting and talking. Ashenden took some of the hotel's notepaper and began to write a letter. When he had finished, he fixed a stamp to the envelope and went to post it. The address on the envelope was:

Chief Inspector Morse
Thames Valley Police Headquarters
Kidlington
Oxford

12

The Suitcase

Cedric Downes was in the Interview Room at St Aldate's
Police Station. Morse sat down in the chair opposite
him.

'Tell me about Dr Kemp,' he said.

'Tell you what? Everybody knows about Kemp. He had
more love affairs than anyone else in Oxford,' replied
Downes. 'He was a horrible man.'

'You say that "everybody" knows?' asked Morse.

'Yes. Including his wife. She knows.'

'Knew, sir. Marion Kemp died this afternoon.'

'Oh.' Downes closed his eyes. 'I know what you're going to
ask me now, Inspector. You're going to ask me if my wife had
an affair with Kemp. Well, the answer is no. She told me that
Kemp had once suggested to her that they make love. But she
had refused. Kemp's behaviour made me very angry,' said
Downes, his eyes shining with hate.

'What did you hit him with?' asked Morse. 'When you
went home for – for whatever it was —'

'What did you say?' said Downes.

'You put your key into the front door, and then when you went in —'

'Yes, I got my spare hearing-aid.'

'Where do you keep your spare hearing-aid?' asked Morse.

'In our bedroom,' replied Downes.

'All right,' said Morse. 'You went upstairs to the bedroom and saw your wife in bed —'

'But my wife *wasn't* in bed. This was at lunchtime!'

'Where was she, then?'

'I don't know. In the sitting-room, I think. Why don't you ask her?'

At that moment, there was a knock at the door and Lewis came in. He was looking very shocked and upset.

'Can I talk to you alone, sir?' he asked Morse. 'It's very urgent.'

Morse went out of the room with the Sergeant.

'The police in London have phoned,' said Lewis. 'Mrs Downes has had an accident. She was knocked down by a car at about half-past five, near Paddington Station. She's in a hospital there, but she's not badly injured.

'The London police said that she stepped off the pavement, in front of a car,' he continued. 'She didn't check whether it was safe to cross the road.'

Morse sighed. 'Was this really an accident, Lewis?' he said. 'Perhaps she was pushed.'

'But why do you say that, sir?' asked Lewis. 'Why would anybody push her?'

Morse was silent for a moment. Then he asked, 'Did she have her suitcase with her at the time of the accident?'

'I don't know, sir,' replied Lewis.

'Listen, Lewis,' said Morse. 'I want you to drive to London now and see Mrs Downes in the hospital. Find out from her exactly what happened. And find that suitcase. I want to know what was inside it.'

<hr>

Janet Roscoe and Shirley Brown were sitting together in Janet's hotel room in Stratford. They had eaten their dinner, and now they were talking for a while before bedtime. They were talking about John Ashenden.

'Have you noticed how quiet Mr Ashenden has been all day?' Shirley Brown asked Janet. 'Perhaps something is worrying him.'

'Yes,' replied Janet. 'And I think that I know what it is. I noticed that Mr Ashenden was writing a letter in the hotel lounge this evening. And when he put the letter down on the table, I saw who it was addressed to. It was addressed to Chief Inspector Morse!'

'Really?' said Shirley. She was very surprised. 'But why was he writing to Chief Inspector Morse? You notice everything, Janet,' she added.

Janet smiled. 'I notice most things,' she said quietly.

<hr>

After Lewis had left for London, Morse went back to Cedric Downes in the Interview Room. But the interview was not going very well. Downes would not agree with anything that Morse said.

'You're a very clever man, Mr Downes,' said Morse. 'You killed a man and covered up[54] the murder. You killed Dr Kemp and you put his body in the River Cherwell. Then you put his clothes in a suitcase and told your wife to take the suitcase to London. Where did she leave the suitcase? Did she leave it at Paddington Station?'

'You're mad, Inspector,' said Downes. 'I don't know what you're talking about. I didn't do *any* of those things!'

<hr>

Less than two hours after he had left Oxford, Sergeant Lewis was at the hospital where Lucy Downes was being looked after. He was talking to a nurse.

The nurse told Lewis that Mrs Downes was very lucky. A car had hit her, but she was not badly hurt.

Lewis went into Lucy's room. Lucy was lying awake in bed.

'Hello, Mrs Downes,' he said. 'How are you?'

'Hello, Sergeant,' said Lucy. 'I'm much better now. But is Cedric coming here soon? I want to see him. Does he know that I've had an accident?'

'Don't worry about that, Mrs Downes,' replied Lewis. 'We'll look after your husband.' He did not want to tell her that Downes was under arrest in the Oxford City police station.

'How did the accident happen, Mrs Downes?' Lewis asked.

'Oh, it was my fault completely,' said Lucy. 'I was in a hurry to get to the station to catch my train. I stepped off the pavement and a car knocked me down. It wasn't the driver's fault – it was mine. I didn't check that it was safe to cross the street. But the car hit my suitcase before it hit me. The suitcase saved me from being more seriously hurt.'

'Do you know where the case is now, Mrs Downes?' Lewis asked.

'Yes,' said Lucy. 'It's here, under the bed.'

———

Five minutes later, Lewis phoned Morse.

'Mrs Downes is going to be all right,' he said. 'She isn't badly hurt. And I have some news about the suitcase. I opened the case. Guess what was inside. New curtains – *not* Kemp's clothes! When Mrs Downes told us that she was taking her curtains to London, she was telling us the truth!'

———

'How did the accident happen, Mrs Downes?'

After he had finished speaking to Lewis, Morse had a lot to think about. He had been wrong about what was in the suitcase – it contained only curtains. So did that mean that he was wrong about Cedric Downes as well?

It was getting late. Morse knew that he was very tired and that he should go home to sleep. But four ideas were going round and round in his mind.

One – there must be a connection between the theft of the Wolvercote Tongue and Theodore Kemp's murder.

Two – more than one person must have been involved in the crimes, especially in the murder.

Three – somewhere among all the evidence, there was an important fact that Morse had missed.

Four – although he had been wrong about the suitcase, he was somehow right about Cedric Downes. Downes really *was* the murderer.

Morse could not know it then, but three of his four ideas were correct.

———

Saturday had been a very long day for Inspector Morse and Sergeant Lewis. They had interviewed many people, and they had arrested a man for murder. But Morse had had to release Cedric Downes from the police station because there was no evidence against him.

It was two o'clock on Sunday morning when Morse finally went to bed. He slept for twelve hours, and he did no more work on Sunday.

13

The Wrong Name

It was late afternoon on Monday. The tour group had left Stratford-upon-Avon after lunch, and the coach was now approaching the historic city of Bath. It was a beautiful autumn day and everybody in the group was feeling happier. And Ashenden was feeling much better than he had felt in Oxford. As the coach entered Bath, he turned on his microphone and began talking about the history of the city.

'This is a lovely place, honey,' said Howard Brown to his wife.

'Yes,' replied Shirley. 'But I wish Laura and Eddie were here to see it with us. The bus seems empty without them.'

Phil Aldrich and Janet Roscoe were still not speaking to each other. As usual, Phil sat at the back of the coach and Janet sat at the front, in the seat behind John Ashenden. Ashenden was telling the group about the many famous English writers who had visited Bath. Janet Roscoe took a book by Jane Austen out of her handbag and began to read. She smiled sweetly at Ashenden.

'Yes,' the tour leader thought, 'our visit to Bath is going to be a success.'

———

On Tuesday morning, Lewis went to talk to Morse in the inspector's office. He told Morse that Lucy Downes was still in hospital, but that she was getting better.

Morse was not happy. He was no closer to solving either the murder or the theft. And now there was another piece of evidence which did not really help him. When Lewis entered the office, Morse was holding an envelope in his hand. It had been posted in Stratford-upon-Avon. He took out two sheets of paper and handed them to Lewis.

'This is a letter from Ashenden,' he said. 'Read it, Lewis. He's a man who likes pornographic[55] videos. He isn't a murderer!'

Lewis read the letter.

The Swan Hotel
Stratford-upon-Avon
Saturday, 3rd November

Dear Inspector

I've been very worried since I left Oxford because I didn't tell you the whole truth. What I told you about the phone call which Kemp made from London was correct. But I lied about where I was on Friday afternoon. You kept my betting-slip and you probably know by now that the horse I bet on won the race. And you know that I did not stay in the betting shop to collect my money.

I wanted people to think that I had been in Summertown because I did not want anyone to know where I really was. In fact, I was in a flat in another part of Oxford most of Friday afternoon. I was watching pornographic videos. I was with three other people. One of them has agreed to talk to you, and he will tell you that this is the truth. I'm sorry that I lied to you – I did not want anybody to know that I like that kind of video. I might lose my job if anyone from the tour company finds out about this.

Also, I did not tell you the whole truth about what I did when we first arrived in Oxford on Thursday. I did not tell you that I went to the Holywell Cemetery. When I was a young man, I had a good friend in Oxford. His name was James Bowden. We lost touch with each other and he died nine years ago. Before he died, he wrote to me, but I did not reply to his letter. I have always been sad about this, and I wanted to visit his grave in the Holywell Cemetery. I wanted to tell him that I was sorry. I know that this sounds stupid, so I did not want to tell you about it.

Now I've told you the whole truth. I'm sorry if I've made your job more difficult. Please collect my money from the betting shop and give it to a hospital, to help people who are ill.

John Ashenden

'So now we know where Ashenden really was on Friday afternoon,' said Lewis. 'We'll check on his alibi, sir, but I don't think that he killed Kemp either.

'There's something else too,' Lewis continued. 'Yesterday I went to the Railway Centre in Didcot. Eddie Stratton told us that he was there on Friday, the afternoon that Kemp was killed. One of the people who works there remembered him. He took a photo of Stratton, and Stratton asked him to send a copy of the photo to his address in America.'

'Did you see the photo?' asked Morse.

'Yes, I got it printed immediately. The photo was certainly of Eddie Stratton. He was there in Didcot for most of the afternoon. So he couldn't have killed Kemp either.'

'There's something I don't understand,' said Morse slowly. 'Kemp phoned the Randolph Hotel from London at about twelve thirty-five. He said that he was phoning from Paddington Station. He said that he had missed the twelve thirty train to Oxford and that he would take the one thirty train. But if you look at the train timetable, you can see that there were trains to Oxford before one thirty. There was a train at twelve forty-five. If Kemp was already at Paddington station, why didn't he take the twelve forty-five train? Why did he wait for the train at one thirty? And why —'

Suddenly Morse stopped.

'What a fool I've been!' he said angrily. 'What's the name of Kemp's publishers? Didn't you phone them to check that Kemp really had been there that morning?'

'Yes – the company is called Babbington's,' replied Lewis.

'That's right,' said Morse quickly. 'And "Babbington's" sounds very like "Paddington". Kemp wasn't phoning from Paddington Station. He was still at his publishers' office, in another part of London. He was really phoning from Babbington's, but Ashenden thought that he said "Paddington".'

Morse's blue eyes were shining with excitement.

'Lewis, I think I know what happened now. Contact the American Consulate[56] in London! Quickly! Find out where Eddie Stratton is. Somebody at the Consulate will know, because he's arranged to take a body back to America. We've got to stop him leaving Britain.'

———

But Eddie Stratton and his dead wife, Laura, had already left Britain on a flight for New York the previous evening.

14

A Clever Plan

There were still many things which Morse had to find out. He gave instructions to Lewis, to Sergeant Dixon and to several other police officers.

Lewis phoned the publishers, Babbington's, in London. He found out that Kemp had not left their offices until about twelve thirty on the day he was murdered. So Morse had been right. Kemp had made the phone call from Babbington's, not from Paddington.

Morse had told Sergeant Dixon to phone all the car hire companies in Oxford. He wanted information about the hire of a car on the afternoon when Kemp had died.

The other police officers had to make calls to America. They made many phone calls to state governments[57], police departments and other addresses.

Morse phoned the police in New York himself. He asked them to arrest Mr Eddie Stratton as soon as his plane landed at JFK Airport[58]. After the police had arrested Stratton, Morse spoke to him for a long time on the phone. He learnt some very interesting things.

———

The next morning, Morse and Lewis travelled to the Chesterton Hotel in Bath, where the American group was staying.

When they arrived, the tourists and John Ashenden were sitting together in one of the large downstairs rooms in the hotel. They were listening to a talk on the history of Bath. Mrs Janet Roscoe was sitting in the front row of seats, while Phil Aldrich sat at the back.

As Morse and Lewis walked into the room, everybody stared at them in surprise.

'I'm sorry to interrupt your talk,' Morse told the group, 'but I have some very important things to tell you.'

There was complete silence in the room as Morse spoke.

'Last Thursday,' he went on, 'Mrs Laura Stratton died from a heart attack. At the same time, a famous and important jewel – the Wolvercote Tongue – was stolen from her room at the Randolph Hotel in Oxford. The jewel was insured for a lot of money. If it was lost or stolen, the insurance company had to pay the Strattons half a million dollars. Eddie Stratton told me this when I spoke to him yesterday in America.'

'But Eddie didn't steal the jewel,' said Janet Roscoe. 'He was out walking with Shirley Brown when it disappeared.'

'Please, Mrs Roscoe, let me continue,' said Morse. 'The Wolvercote Tongue was stolen, Laura Stratton died, and the next day Dr Theodore Kemp was murdered. From the beginning of the murder investigation, I was sure that there was a connection between these events. "Did the person who stole the jewel also murder Dr Kemp?" I asked myself.

'Kemp was the victim of two crimes. First, he – or the museum where he worked – was robbed of[59] the jewel. Then he was robbed of his life. Who hated Kemp enough to do these things?

'Two years ago, Dr Kemp was involved in a terrible car crash. He wasn't hurt, but his wife was seriously injured and she spent the rest of her life in a wheelchair. The driver of the other car – a woman called Mrs Mayo – was killed. Mrs Mayo was from California.

'It was not proved that Theodore Kemp was responsible for the accident,' Morse went on. 'But Kemp *had* been driving the car and he *had* been drinking. Because of that, his driving licence was taken away and he had to pay a large fine. But he still had his life, not like the dead woman, Mrs Mayo.

'How does this connect with the crimes which were committed last week? Kemp phoned the Randolph Hotel from London at about twelve thirty on Friday. Kemp told Mr Ashenden that he would arrive at Oxford Station at three o'clock, and Ashenden arranged for a taxi to collect him. Dr Kemp *did* arrive in Oxford at three o'clock. But he didn't take the taxi. Why? Because somebody else – somebody that knew Kemp – had met him at the railway station. They had picked him up in a car and they had driven him away.'

Janet Roscoe opened her mouth to speak again, but Morse

went on. 'I now know that somebody went to a car hire company in North Oxford early on Friday afternoon. They arranged to hire a car. Then they drove the hired car to the railway station and they picked up Dr Kemp. But who was this person? It wasn't Mr Eddie Stratton or Mr Howard Brown. Mr Stratton was on his way to Didcot, and Mr Brown was meeting an old friend. We've checked both their alibis. Both men are telling the truth.'

Shirley Brown looked at her husband in surprise.

'What about your tour leader?' said Morse. Ashenden was looking down, staring at the floor. 'No, it wasn't him either. Mr Ashenden was in Summertown for the afternoon with some – some friends. We've checked his alibi too.

'But now we come to Mr Phil Aldrich.' Everybody turned round to look at the small man sitting quietly in the back row. 'Mr Aldrich said that he went to London that afternoon. He said that he travelled back on the train which Mr Stratton got onto at Didcot. And Mr Stratton told us that he saw Mr Aldrich on the train.

'But *somebody* hired a car and met Dr Theodore Kemp at the railway station at three o'clock. It wasn't Mrs Sheila Williams and it wasn't Mr Cedric Downes – they were both with people from this tour party at that time. But somebody did go to the station to meet Dr Kemp. And it was one of *you*. It was somebody in this room!'

———

While Morse was talking to the tour group in Bath, four police officers were swimming in the river that runs through the small village of Wolvercote, near Oxford. These divers were searching the bottom of the river for something very special. They knew exactly where to look because Morse's instructions had been very clear.

In his phone conversation with Morse, Eddie Stratton

had told the inspector that he'd thrown the Wolvercote Tongue into the river. He had described the exact place where he had been standing when he threw it – the small bridge over the river at Wolvercote.

The police divers spent all morning searching the river, but without success. By the afternoon they still had not found the jewel.

Meanwhile, Eddie Stratton was at JFK Airport in New York, waiting for a flight back to Britain. An American police officer was with him, in case he tried to escape. But Stratton did not want to escape. He wanted to talk to Morse again – there were things that he wanted to tell the inspector.

———

In the hotel in Bath, Morse continued to talk to the tour group.

'Somebody met Kemp at Oxford Station on Friday afternoon and drove him to his own flat in Water Eaton Road. I think that there was a quarrel in Kemp's sitting-room. During the quarrel, Kemp was struck on the head. He fell, hit the back of his head on the fireplace and died. I think that Kemp died at about three forty-five.

'Kemp's wife, Marion, was at home when her husband died, so why didn't she call the police? I'm sure that she was there all the time. But I think that she hated Kemp and that she wasn't sorry about his death. He had ruined her life in that car accident. Perhaps Mrs Kemp didn't call the police because she wanted to protect the person, or the people, who were quarrelling with her husband. Perhaps she already knew that somebody else would meet her husband at the station and bring him home. Perhaps she knew that there would be a quarrel.'

'Inspector, you are talking nonsense!' said Janet Roscoe suddenly.

'Inspector, you are talking nonsense!' said Janet Roscoe.

Morse took no notice of Mrs Roscoe. 'At about seven o'clock that evening, when it was dark, somebody came to the flat to remove Kemp's body. That person removed the dead man's clothes, took his body outside to the garden and put it in a wheelbarrow. Then they pushed the wheelbarrow down to the river and put Kemp's naked body into the water.

'The person who did that was somebody from your group. It was a person who is used to undressing and moving dead bodies because that is his job. He is a professional mortician. In fact, it was Mr Eddie Stratton.'

'No, sir!'

Somebody had called out from the back of the room. Everybody looked round in surprise. It was Phil Aldrich.

'Please let me explain, Mr Aldrich,' said Morse. 'Eddie and Laura Stratton had been married for two years. But they had a very expensive way of life. They had spent all Laura's money from her dead husband, and now they had very little money for themselves.

'But Laura knew that the Wolvercote Tongue was insured for half a million dollars. So the Strattons planned to bring the jewel to Oxford, but they also planned for it to be stolen before it could be given to the Ashmolean Museum. They thought that they, not the museum, would receive the insurance money.

'As the Strattons were discussing their plan on the coach, somebody overheard their conversation – a person with very good hearing, a person who notices everything. This person learnt that the Strattons were planning to "steal" the jewel themselves.

'This person made an agreement with the Strattons. This person offered to steal the jewel, so that nobody would suspect the Strattons of the theft. But in return, Eddie Stratton would have to do something. He did not know what it was, but he had to agree. If he didn't agree, the person would tell the police the truth about the theft. Then the Strattons would lose half a million dollars.

'When Laura Stratton went to her room at the Randolph Hotel, she left her handbag with the jewel near the open door. It was very easy for somebody to take the bag. Eddie Stratton had gone out for a walk with Mrs Shirley Brown. So nobody could accuse him of stealing the jewel.

'Everything seemed to be going well. But then something went wrong. Laura Stratton had a heart attack and died in the room.'

Morse stopped talking and looked at his watch.

'Mr Eddie Stratton has given me a lot of very interesting information. But I need to talk to him again. He is at this moment under arrest and he's flying back to London from New York. Stratton *didn't* steal the jewel or murder Kemp. But he knew about the theft and about the murder. And he was the person who put Kemp's body into the River Cherwell. That is what he had agreed to do.

'Mr Stratton has refused to tell me the name of the person who hit Dr Kemp on the head. But I'm going to find out who it was – and I'm going to find out very soon!'

15

The Jewel That Was Lost

Eddie Stratton was on the plane flying across the Atlantic to Heathrow Airport in London. There was a New York police officer sitting silently beside him.

Stratton was thinking about all the things that had

happened in Oxford. Everything had been Laura's fault. Laura always spoke in a very loud voice. It was not surprising that somebody on the coach had overheard them talking about their plan to steal the Wolvercote Tongue – 'the jewel that is ours' as Laura had often called it.

The surprising thing was that this person wanted the Wolvercote Tongue to be stolen too! This person hated Theodore Kemp and wanted to make trouble for him at the museum where he worked. They knew how unhappy Kemp would be when the jewel was stolen.

It had been easy to arrange for the jewel to disappear. They had all agreed on the plan the night before they came to Oxford. Laura would complain about her feet and go up to her hotel room. She would leave her handbag near the open door so that it could be stolen easily.

Stratton himself had to stay away from the hotel while the jewel was stolen. He had to go out for a walk with one of the other people on the tour. Afterwards, the person who stole the jewel would give it to him. Stratton would then make sure that it would never be found.

And that is what had happened. Stratton had thrown the Tongue into the river at Wolvercote. But before he'd done this, he'd removed the large valuable ruby. Nobody knew that the ruby was now in New York, hidden under his dead wife's body.

Stratton had not had anything to do with his wife's death. But what about the second death – Theodore Kemp's death? That was different. He knew a lot about that. But he was never going to tell anybody exactly how Kemp had died – especially not Chief Inspector Morse.

The hotel room in Bath suddenly seemed very hot. Howard Brown was wiping his face with a large handkerchief.

Ashenden brushed the sleeve of his jacket across his lips.

'I know who stole the Wolvercote Tongue,' Morse said quietly. 'I know where it is, and I am sure that it will soon be found. And I know which of you were at Dr Kemp's house when he died.'

There was a long silence. Nobody in the room moved. Morse stood still, his eyes moving to the left and to the right as he looked along the group.

'All right,' said Morse. 'There isn't much more to tell you. But the reason for Kemp's death was that road accident. Kemp killed the driver of the other car – a thirty-five-year-old woman from California. Her name was Mrs Philippa Mayo.

'Yesterday, I found out a lot about Philippa Mayo. Her husband had died some years before she did. She was an only child. Her parents had loved her very much. So how did her parents feel when she was killed in a stupid road accident? When she was killed by a selfish, drunk man called Theodore Kemp? A man who wasn't really punished for causing her death? A man who didn't even have to go to prison?

'Philippa's parents were very angry that Kemp had not been punished for their daughter's death. So they decided to come over to England to meet him themselves. They hated Kemp because he had killed their daughter, and they decided that he should know that. Perhaps they would decide that he had to die too.

'But who are these people – this man and his wife?' Morse said. He looked around the room. 'When I read the questionnaires that everybody in this group had filled in, I found that two people lived in the same apartment building in California. But they had not come on the tour as man and wife.

'Eddie Stratton was certainly at Didcot on the afternoon that Kemp was killed. But he lied about his train journey back to Oxford. He said that he saw Phil Aldrich on that train. But Phil Aldrich was *not* on the train from London to Oxford that afternoon. He was in Oxford already – he had been arguing with Dr Theodore Kemp.

'Mr Aldrich told me that he went to London to see his daughter, Pippa, that afternoon,' went on Morse. 'But that was impossible. His daughter, Pippa, or Philippa, was already dead. She was killed two years ago by Theodore Kemp. Philippa Mayo was your daughter, wasn't she, Mr Aldrich?'

'Are you serious about all this, sir?' asked Phil Aldrich.

'Oh, yes,' said Morse quietly. 'I'm sorry, Mr Aldrich. You don't have a daughter in London. And Mr Stratton has now told me the truth – he didn't see you on the train.

'We've been talking to the police department in your home town. And we've talked with your neighbours, and with your daughter's school. We've checked your home address. There's no doubt about the facts.

'But what about your wife, Mr Aldrich? She didn't give us all the details of her address on the questionnaire. She told us that she lives in the same town, the same street, the same apartment building as you. But she didn't tell us that she lives in the same apartment. But we know now that you've been married to this lady for forty-two years.

'When she was young, your wife was a well-known actress. Her stage name – the name which she used as an actress – was Janet Roscoe. That's the name she used on this tour too. And Philippa Mayo's name, before she got married, was Philippa Janet Aldrich.'

Phil Aldrich got up from his seat at the back of the room and walked to the front. He sat in the seat beside Janet Roscoe and she smiled at him.

Phil Aldrich put his hand gently on Janet's arm. There were tears running down his cheeks. Janet turned to him. In

Phil Aldrich put his hand gently on Janet's arm.

her eyes, Morse could see a deep love. They were the eyes of a mother whose sadness could never be changed. They were the eyes of a woman who had travelled to England to meet the man who had killed her daughter – the man who had killed 'the jewel that was hers'.

————

Morse took statements from Phil and Janet Aldrich, and from Eddie Stratton when he arrived from New York. Then, for Morse, the case was finished.

Everything had happened as Morse had described. The Aldriches had seen Dr Theodore Kemp's name when they read the advertisement for the Historic England Tour. They recognised him as the same Dr Kemp who had killed their daughter.

Janet Roscoe was very ill and she was not going to live for much longer. She wanted to meet – and punish – Theodore Kemp before she died herself. So the Aldriches had joined the tour. And on the coach, Janet had overheard the Strattons discussing how they were going to steal the Wolvercote Tongue. Janet and Phil had offered their help because they knew that the theft of the jewel would damage Kemp's career. And the Aldriches also thought that Eddie Stratton could help them get rid of the body, if they decided to *kill* Kemp.

So Janet took the Wolvercote Tongue from Laura Stratton's hotel room in the Randolph Hotel. Later, she gave it to Eddie Stratton.

The next day, Janet overheard Kemp's phone call to Ashenden, and immediately she and Phil made their plans. Eddie Stratton was sent to Didcot for the afternoon to give him an alibi. Phil went to hire a car, and later picked up Janet. Then they both went to the station to meet Kemp.

The Aldriches told Kemp that his wife was ill, and that

they would drive him to his flat. There, somebody hit Kemp on the front of the head with his wife's walking stick. Kemp fell, hit the back of his head against a corner of the fire-place, and died.

Who had attacked Kemp with the walking stick? Was it Phil Aldrich? Was it his wife Janet? Or was it Marion Kemp herself? Morse never found out which of them had done it. The Aldriches would not tell him and Marion Kemp was dead. But all of them had hated Kemp. All of them had wanted to punish the man who had ruined their lives.

When Stratton returned from Didcot, Janet told him to go to the Kemps' flat. There, Stratton took the clothes from the dead man's body and carried the body to the river.

After leaving the Kemps' flat in Water Eaton Road, Stratton had walked to the village of Wolvercote. There, he had thrown the jewel into the river. Then he walked back into Oxford, where he had met Sheila Williams. He had gone home with her and had drunk a lot of whisky.

———

'Marion Kemp was an amazing woman,' said Lewis, when he was talking to Morse the next morning. 'She stayed in her bedroom all that afternoon, alone with her husband's dead body.'

'She could never forgive her husband,' said Morse. 'Kemp had ruined her life. But after his death, she had no one to look after her. She was a very unhappy woman, and in the end she killed herself.'

'Do you think that the police divers will find the jewel in the river?' asked Lewis.

'I hope so,' said Morse sadly. 'But the Aldriches will never get *their* jewel back, will they? The jewel that was theirs – their daughter.'

———

Later that day, Morse went to Holywell Cemetery where Ashenden's friend was buried. He didn't need to know whether the tour leader had told him the truth about his visit to the cemetery. But he wanted to go there.

At the cemetery, Morse found the poem which Ashenden had put beside the small tombstone for his friend.

> *Life took us from each other,*
> *Taking friend from friend.*
> *I bring this goodbye now, with my tears.*
> *It is all I have to bring.*

POINTS
FOR
UNDERSTANDING
and
GLOSSARY

Points for Understanding

1

Do you think that Howard and Shirley Brown have a good relationship? Find some sentences which give you information about this.

2

Morse asks Sheila Williams where she was between 4.30 and 5.15 p.m. She replies, 'Ask Dr Kemp – he'll explain!' Why do you think that she says this?

3

'Perhaps the Wolvercote Tongue ... never left America!' Morse thinks. Why does he think this?

4

When Kemp tried to get better jobs at the University, he was unsuccessful. But his colleagues think that he is lucky. Why do they think this?

5

Morse learns that Ashenden has lied to him about what he was doing the previous afternoon. What has made Morse suspicious?

6

Sheila Williams's house was comfortable and pleasant. Morse was a little surprised. Why do you think that he is surprised?

7

When Morse writes the questionnaire for the tourists to complete, he includes a question about the date of their arrival in Britain. Why do you think that he does this?

8

'Is Mr Downes in?' Lewis asks Mrs Downes. Why does he ask this?

9

Why does Morse think that Kemp might have been killed at the Downes' house?

10

How does Morse know how much money Ashenden won from his bet?

11

Morse knows several things which make him believe that Cedric Downes murdered Theodore Kemp. Write down three of these things.

12

'Mrs Downes was telling us the truth,' Lewis tells Morse when he finds new curtains in her suitcase. Why might he be wrong about this?

13

Why is this chapter called 'The Wrong Name'?

14

'The Strattons thought that they, not the museum, would receive the insurance money,' says Morse. Why would they think this?

15

'Eddie Stratton was sent to Didcot ... to give him an alibi,' Morse says. Why was Eddie's need for an alibi greater than Janet Roscoe's?

Glossary

1 **tourists** (page 6)
visitors to a country who travel round it, to look at its famous places. A group of visitors who do this together are on a *tour*. The person who makes the arrangements for the group, and travels with them, is the *tour leader*.

2 **lecturers** (page 8)
teachers at a university or a college.

3 **affair** (page 9)
if you have a sexual relationship with someone who you are not married to, you are having an *affair* with that person.

4 **Stratford-upon-Avon** (page 9)
a small town, in the centre of England, where the famous writer William Shakespeare was born. Many tourists visit the house where Shakespeare was born, and the famous theatre where his plays are performed. Although the full name of the town is sometimes used, people often simply call it 'Stratford'.

5 **arthritis** (page 10)
an illness which makes the joints between the bones of your body painful.

6 **honey** (page 10)
Americans often call people that they love, *honey*. Honey is a very sweet liquid, and if you call someone this, it means that you think that he or she is a sweet person.

7 **architecture** (page 10)
the way a building is designed is called its *architecture*.

8 **reception desk** (page 10)
the place, near the main door of a hotel, where you give your name and collect your room key when you arrive. This is also where you pay your bill when you leave the hotel. Someone who works at this desk is called a *receptionist*.

9 **DO NOT DISTURB sign** (page 12)
a piece of card with the words 'DO NOT DISTURB' printed on it. There is one in every hotel room. If you want to stay in your hotel room, and you do not want anyone else to come in, you hang this piece of card, or *sign*, on the outside of your door.

10 **bubble bath** (page 12)
a liquid which you add to the water in a bath. The liquid makes bubbles in the water and has a pleasant smell.

11 **tombstone** (page 13)

a *tomb* is another word for a grave – a place where a dead body is buried. A *tombstone* is a piece of stone, placed in the ground over the grave, on which words are carved. These words tell you the name of the person who is buried and the dates of their birth and death.

12 **lost touch** – *to lose touch with* (page 13)

if you stop meeting, writing to, or phoning somebody that you know, you *lose touch with* that person. You can say that two people have *lost touch*. You do not need to add 'with each other'.

13 **theft** (page 14)

if something is stolen, there has been a *theft* of that thing. A person who steals something is called a *thief*. There is also a verb, *to thieve*, meaning *to steal*, but it is rarely used now.

14 **cases** (page 15)

an investigation into a crime is sometimes called a *case*. A *case* is also a container for something – for example, a brief*case* and a suit*case* are often just called a case. The same word is often used for a doctor's treatment of somebody's illness, but in this book only the first of these two meanings is used.

15 **heart attack** (page 15)

if your heart suddenly stops working properly, or if it stops working completely, you have had a *heart attack*. People often die from heart attacks.

16 **evidence** (page 16)

the things and facts which are discovered during the investigation of a crime.

17 **pathologist** (page 16)

a doctor who looks carefully at, or *examines*, dead bodies, to find out how people have died. A pathologist can do many tests on a body, which provide evidence for the police detectives who are investigating an unusual death or a murder.

18 **stretch their legs** – *to stretch your legs* (page 16)

if you have been sitting in one place for a long time, the joints in your legs might have become stiff. If you then get up and walk around for a while, to exercise your joints, you are *stretching your legs*.

19 **artefact** (page 20)

the meaning of *artefact* here is 'something which was made a long time ago, and something which is important for understanding people who lived at that time'. The thing which is described here is a *jewel*. 'Jewel' means here, a beautiful object made from valuable materials – gold, precious stones, etc. It does *not* mean a single precious stone, although the word sometimes means that in English. The jewel in this story was one part of a pair of fastenings – a buckle and tongue. They might have been attached to the ends of pieces of leather or fabric, such as belts, cloak-fastenings, etc. The buckle is a small frame of metal or bone which is fixed to one part of the fastening, or one end of a belt. The tongue is another piece of metal or bone, usually rounded or pointed, which is on the other part of the fastening or the other end of the belt. The tongue fits into the buckle.

Although the pair of jewels described in this book are not real, the Ashmolean Museum does have a beautiful ninth-century artefact called the Alfred Jewel, named after King Alfred (849-899). It was the Alfred Jewel which gave Colin Dexter the idea for this book.

20 **rubies** (page 20)
red-coloured precious stones. Large rubies are very valuable.

21 **antiquities** (page 20)
things which were made a very long time ago. Things which people collect and which are only a few hundred years old are usually called *antiques*. The different word, *antiquities*, is only used to describe things which have existed for a thousand years, two thousand years, or more.

22 **will** (page 20)
if you write down your instructions about who you want to have your money, and the other things that you own, after your death, you are making your *will*.

23 **ceremony** (page 21)
Mrs Stratton was going to give – or *present* – the jewel to the museum. This *presentation* was going to happen at an important meeting with many people watching. A presentation is a type of

ceremony. When *present* is a verb, the second syllable is stressed. But when it is a noun, the first syllable is stressed. The word *presentation* is stressed on the third syllable.

24 **briefcase** (page 22)
a small case used for carrying papers and documents.

25 **undertaker** (page 24)
a person who prepares dead bodies for their funerals, and who makes all the arrangements for these funerals, is called an *undertaker* in Britain. In America, this person is usually called a *mortician*.

26 **insured** (page 26)
if you *have insurance* on something or somebody, you pay money to an *insurance company* every year, or every month, to *insure* that thing or person. You can insure a building, a painting, any other valuable object, or you can insure somebody's life. If the thing is then lost, stolen, damaged or destroyed, or if the person dies or is killed, you *make a claim* to the insurance company. The company pays you money to repair or replace the thing, or to help you after the death of the person.

27 **wheelchair** (page 27)
a chair, usually made of metal, which has wheels. A person who cannot walk uses a wheelchair to move around. There are usually four wheels – two small ones at the front, next to the person's feet, and two large ones next to the seat. The person usually moves the chair by pushing the large wheels round, although some wheelchairs are powered by electricity.

28 **fine** (page 27)
if a court of law finds you guilty of a crime, you receive a punishment. For serious crimes, you are usually sent to prison. For less serious crimes, you often have to pay an amount of money to the government. This amount of money is called a *fine*.

29 **colleagues** (page 28)
people who work with you.

30 **suspected** (page 28)
if you think that somebody has done something but you do not know this for certain, you *suspect* them of doing it. You are *suspicious of* them. And if something seems strange to you, and you are worried about it, you are *suspicious about* it. You can simply say that that thing is *suspicious*. But if you say that a person is *suspicious*, you mean 'He suspects somebody of something', *not* 'I suspect him of something'. If the police arrest someone that they

think has done something wrong, they arrest him *on suspicion of* doing it.

31 **suspicious** (page 35)
see Glossary number 30.

32 **Parson's Pleasure** (page 37)
for many years, this part of the River Cherwell has had high walls around its banks. Men can swim naked here if they wish to. A *parson* is an old word for a clergyman or priest. The name 'Parson's Pleasure' is a joke.

33 **weir** (page 37)
a small man-made waterfall, where a river changes its level, and where the flow of its water can be controlled.

34 **wounds** (page 38)
a *wound* is an injury to the surface of a body – usually a cut or hole in the skin.

35 **identity card** (page 40)
a card which shows your name and other details about you, usually together with a photograph of you. It proves that you are the person who you say you are. All policemen must carry an identity card, which they must show to people before they interview them.

36 **walking stick** (page 41)
a strong, straight wooden stick or metal pole, which some people use to help them walk. They can rest some of their weight on the stick rather than on their legs.

37 **good taste** (page 42)
your *tastes* are the types of thing you like. For example, the clothes you like, the way your house is decorated, the music you listen to, the books you read, etc. If all the things you like are things which people agree are of high quality, you have *good taste*.

38 **continental Europe** (page 45)
the countries which form the large area of land – the *continent* – of Europe. Although Britain and Ireland are also part of Europe, they are large islands, and not areas of the continent.

39 **questionnaire** (page 46)
a printed form containing questions, which is given to a number of people to complete. Although *questionnaire* is really a French word, the 'qu' is usually now pronounced in the English way.

40 **phone attachment** (page 48)
an *attachment* is something which is fixed, or *attached*, to something else. Downes has an attachment which is fixed to his phone, and which makes the sound that comes from it louder.

41 **mortuary** (page 50)

a room, usually in a hospital, where the bodies of people who have died are kept. Pathologists examine bodies in a mortuary.

42 **skull** (page 50)

the bones of your head.

43 **mortician** (page 50)

see Glossary number 25.

44 **Paddington Station** (page 53)

London has many large railway stations where trains begin and end their journeys to and from different parts of Britain. Paddington Station is the station for trains travelling to the west of England and to Wales. Trains to Oxford start from this station.

45 **motive** (page 57)

the reason why somebody does something is their *motive* for doing it. For example, if you attack someone and steal their money, your *motive* for attacking them is theft.

46 **stationed** (page 61)

when a member of a country's army or air force lives and works in a place, he is *stationed* there.

47 **King's Cross** (page 61)

the area of London around King's Cross Station – the station for trains travelling to the north-east of England and to Scotland.

48 **Summertown** (page 64)

an area of north Oxford about two kilometres from the city centre. There are many shops there.

49 **betting shop** (page 65)

a kind of shop where you can bet money on a sport, for example horse racing. If you bet on a horse, you have guessed that that horse will win its race, and you give the betting shop some money as your bet. Then if that horse does win the race, the shop gives you your money back and some extra money too. This extra amount depends on the *odds* against the horse. If the betting shop decides, at the time when you *place your bet*, that the horse has one chance in six of winning the race, then the odds are six-to-one against the horse. If it does win, the shop pays you six times the amount of money that you bet on the horse. When you place a bet, the details are written on a *betting-slip*, which the shop gives you. You need this piece of paper to claim your money if your horse wins.

50 **coolness** (page 65)

if two people are not friendly, there is a *coolness* between them. They do not argue, but they behave *coolly* towards each other.

51 **wheelbarrow** (page 69)

a kind of box, with a wheel at the front and two handles at the back. It is used by builders, gardeners, etc, to move heavy things.

52 **get rid of it** (page 72)

to *get rid of* something means to remove it, usually with the extra meaning of making sure that it will never be found.

53 **arrest** (page 74)

when the police think that somebody has committed a crime, and that they have evidence to prove this, they *arrest* that person. The person is then *under arrest*, and the police can keep them at a police station and ask them questions.

54 **covered up** – *to cover up* (page 79)

here the meaning is 'to stop anybody finding out about something'. If you know about a crime, but you don't tell the police about it, you are *covering it up*.

55 **pornographic** (page 84)

pornographic pictures and videos show people who are naked, and people who are having sex with each other.

56 **the American Consulate** (page 86)

most countries have *consulates* in other countries. These are places where people who are travelling abroad can get help from their own governments if they have problems. For example, if all their money is stolen, or if somebody they are travelling with dies. The *American Consulate* in London helps Americans who are travelling or staying in Britain.

57 **state governments** (page 87)

although there is a government for the whole country (the *federal* government) each state in the USA has its own governor and government too. These *state governments* have many powers, and they hold lots of information about the people who live in their areas.

58 **JFK Airport** (page 87)

New York's international airport is named after John F. Kennedy, the American president who was murdered in 1963.

59 **robbed of** (page 88)

if something is stolen from you, you are *robbed of* that thing.

Published by Macmillan Heinemann ELT
Between Towns Road, Oxford OX4 3PP
Macmillan Heinemann ELT is an imprint of
Macmillan Publishers Limited
Companies and representatives throughout the world

ISBN 0 333 93449 0

The Jewel That Was Ours © Colin Dexter 1991

First published by Macmillan (1991)

*Colin Dexter asserts his rights to be identified as the author
of the original work*, The Jewel That Was Ours, *of which
this Guided Reader is an adaptation.*

This retold version for Macmillan Guided Readers
Text ©Macmillan Publishers Limited 2002
Design and illustration © Macmillan Publishers Limited 2002
Heinemann is a registered trademark of Reed Educational & Professional Publishing Limited
This version first published 2002

Designed by Sue Vaudin
Illustrated by Maureen Gray
Cover by James Mealing and Buzz Mitchell

Printed in China

2006 2005 2004 2003 2002
10 9 8 7 6 5 4 3 2 1